The Root Of All Evil

The Chronicles of Detective Marcus Rose (Volume 2)

By

A.D. White

A.D. White

www.adwhite.net

ISBN-13: 978-1537167688
ISBN-10: 1537167685

A.D. White

<u>Acknowledgements</u>

Thanks to my wonderful family for supporting me and encouraging me to follow my dream.

All characters are the work of the author's imagination. This book is a work of fiction and not meant to depict real life events.

**Cover Illustration by
D.J. Jackson, HF Productions**

CHAPTERS

Page

A.D. White

Chapter One
Karma

It was a warm summer night in Washington, D.C. Saturday night and Nicholas was taking time out just to relax and enjoy the fruits of his labor. This was his hideaway, where he went when he wanted to be alone. A place that very few people knew about, including his wife. Here he could take time away from all the hustle and bustle of his thriving business.

Being the boss ain't always easy, he thought to himself as he sipped a glass of one hundred year old Brandy. He sat in his overstuffed recliner and peered out at the city through the floor to ceiling windows that covered the entire east wall of his fifteenth story condominium on Massachusetts Avenue in Northwest, D.C.

As he relaxed, Beethoven's "Moonlight Sonata" played softly in the background. The view of the city at night inspired him. All the distinct vibrant lights. He was perched atop the city and looking down, he could tell where the phrase "rat race" came from to describe a busy city. People and cars racing from here to there in such a hurry. It looked like a beautiful kaleidoscope that intertwined the fabric of humanity. Nicholas was on top of the world, and in his eyes this city belonged to him.

He stood up and walked to the window, pressed his forehead against the pane, smiled, then let out a sinister laugh. His future was limitless, so he thought. He had more money than he could possibly spend in his lifetime.

He was thirty-five years old. Handsome, six feet tall with a slim build, clean shaven with short black hair. He had a devoted wife and a mansion in the suburbs. No children, but that was okay with him. Having children would require that he give a damn about someone other than himself. Nicholas had one sibling but they never really learned to share. It was always me, me, me as he trusted very few.

If you stood in his way, he would walk over you, rather than around. If you didn't agree with him, you were simply wrong. All those who opposed him were casualties of war. Those who didn't get out of his way fast enough were collateral damage. He was ruthless in business as only the strong survived. He didn't think that you could get ahead being Mr. Nice Guy. Oh, he was charming, but if you were unfortunate enough to peel away his top layer, what you saw would give you chills.

A knock at the door startled him. No one knew that he was here and the concierge didn't call up and ask if he was receiving guests. "I'm gonna have somebody's ass for this" he mumbled as he opened the door.

Surprised, he asked "what are you doing here and why are you dressed like that?" "You're not going to invite me in," was their reply? Nicholas sighed, turned around and walked away from the door, as if to signal for the person to follow him, which they did as the front door slammed shut.

As Nicholas turned around, he was met with a knife slashing across his throat. His eyes widened to the size of silver dollars as he grasped at his neck in shock. With the realization that he had just been cut, he started to panic causing his heart to beat faster. Blood from his juggler was spurting out of his body with every beat of his heart, painting this once tranquil scenery red. He froze like a statute, unable to move nor talk, though he tried in vain.

Nicholas then felt the knife enter his abdomen with such force as to penetrate deep into his torso. What little breath he had vanished. All he could do is wonder why as his life flashed before his eyes. Nicholas fell face down to the floor as his killer elegantly stepped back and watched him bleed profusely. The killer stood there watching him die, then bent down and stabbed him multiple times in the center of his back while murmuring "die you bastard, die." The killer then got down on hands and knees and whispered in Nicholas' ear "you thought that you could just fuck over everybody and nothing would ever come back to you?"

Nicholas felt cold as his life was rapidly draining from him. He knew that he was going to die. Nothing could save him now, except a miracle, but he also knew that wasn't going to happen. All the wrong that he had done in his life? "Why would God help him now," he wondered? His first instinct was to fight the inevitable as he attempted to grasp at the shoes of his killer. Then he accepted his fate and his body relaxed. Memories of his childhood began to flash through his mind like a picture show. He saw himself as a child walking to school in the snow. He saw the faces of his childhood sweethearts, graduating college and so on.

He began to feel warm all over. As he slipped into unconsciousness he felt the killer kick him in the side and say "Karma, you asshole" as they walked away. Then it all faded to black.

Chapter Two
Promises, Promises

Marcus Rose was one of the brightest minds on the department. An experienced Homicide Detective, the cream of the crop. Handsome, clever, well liked and respected because he got the job done. He closed cases. He took murderers off the street. At the end of the day that's all that really mattered to his superiors.

Marcus loved his job but he learned a long time ago that it wasn't wise to put all your time and energy into your job, while neglecting your family. He learned from others before him that there has to be a happy medium. He always made a point to set aside quality time for his wife and two boys. After all these years, he and Gina still had that fire for one another.

Marcus was a perfectionist on the job, but at home, Gina was the one that made their house a home. They were both old fashioned. He learned how to be a man by watching how lovingly his father treated his mother. His father was dominant and strong and without a doubt wore the pants in the family, but that didn't change the fact that his mother was the glue that held it all together. She was no pushover. She could hand out an ass whipping when dad wasn't home! It was a team effort. Marcus was the head coach and Gina was the assistant coach, raising their two boys to be honest and responsible men was their goal.

Marcus and Gina had been married for twenty-two years and she was the love of his life. She accepted the fact that there would be times when his job came first, but she also knew that there would also be times when family was the priority. It wasn't all gravy. They had their ups and downs just like all married couples, but they both valued what they had and divorce wasn't an option.

Today was Sunday and the plan was to see Denzel Washington's latest movie and then go to dinner. After the movie was over, they walked out hand in hand. "How'd you like the movie," Gina asked? "I loved it. Denzel's a bad dude," Marcus explained. "Most people don't know that this was a television series back in the 80's." "I remember," Gina laughed. Just then, Marcus' work phone rang. "Detective Rose," he answered. Marcus listened, then sighed "okay, I'm on the way," then looked at Gina "I'm sorry babe, got a homicide in a high rise on Mass Avenue and I'm on the bubble this weekend."

"I'll be glad when we can get a whole weekend together without the job calling. I need your time too, Marcus," said an annoyed Gina. "I know babe. This won't last forever. In a few years, I'll be eligible to retire and then you'll be wishing I wasn't home all the time" he laughed. Gina just shook her head in disappointment.

She was used to it by now and knew that this was the life that she had signed up for, but that didn't make it any easier. It could be worse she thought to herself! She had girlfriends that husbands hung out at night doing God knows what. At least she knew where her man was and what he was doing.

"Drop me at home so I can pick up my car. I'll get something to eat by myself. No use in wasting a good babysitter," as she glared into his eyes. Marcus moved in closer and kissed her on the lips "I'm sorry Boo, I'll make it up to you," and then gave her a passionate hug. "Promises, promises," said Gina as she hugged him back. "I love you Marcus, you be careful." "I love you too baby and I will."

A.D. White

Chapter Three
Familiarity Breeds Contempt

As Marcus pulled up to the high rise building, he could see a line of police cars parked out front. Two crime scene technicians got into their truck and drove away. He pulled into the space they had just left. Marcus exited his vehicle "nice neighborhood," he said to himself as he looked around. Walking into the lobby he was greeted by the concierge "can I help you sir?" Marcus removed his wallet from his back pocket and flipped it open "police, where's the scene?" "It's the penthouse Detective, I'll send for the elevator."

"My name is Detective Rose, and you are?" "The name's Stanley Richardson," he replied as he reached out his hand. Marcus shook his hand "Okay Stanley, show me the way." Stanley walked him to the end of the corridor to the elevator used exclusively for the penthouse. He used a key to summons the elevator and once inside entered 666 into the keypad. "Interesting code" Marcus remarked. "Yeah, the owner picked it himself," said Stanley as he stepped out of the elevator. "Let me know if you need anything else Detective." "Will do" as the doors closed taking him to the penthouse. Before the elevator got to the top floor, Marcus reached inside his jacket pocket and pulled out a small plastic bottle of hand sanitizer, squirted some on his hands and rubbed them together vigorously.

As he stepped off the elevator, he was surprised to see that the penthouse took up the entire floor. "Now this is good living," he thought to himself. There was a uniformed officer standing outside of the penthouse door to protect the crime scene. The officer greeted him "Detective Rose." "Hey Smitty," Marcus replied "how's it going?" "I'm doing better than that guy inside" Officer Smith replied. "Always the optimist," said Marcus. How's the wife Smitty? Is she still putting up with your crap" he asked? "Yep, she's a lucky woman" said Officer Smith. Marcus laughed "yeah, she's real fortunate" he said sarcastically.

Marcus opened the door to the penthouse and walked in. "If it ain't Detective Rose. I'm so glad that you took time out of your day to join us" joked his partner Detective Logan Steele. "Bite me Logan," was Marcus' reply. "A little testy today, huh? Gina must have given you the blues about coming in on your day off. You can go back home. I can handle this scene all by myself," Logan joked.

"Yeah, I'll bet the lieutenant would love that," you just got off of his "S" list. (Marcus rarely used profanity). "One day the lieutenant's gonna realize how fortunate he is to have me here," Logan joked. "Yeah Okay, don't hold your breath," Marcus replied.

Detective Second Grade Logan Steele was Marcus' partner. He was six feet five inches in height with a shaved head and goatee. He was streetwise, has a sarcastic sense of humor and a commanding presence. He was a little rough around the edges though.

"Okay Logan, who do we have here" Marcus inquisitively asked as he looked up and saw the body lying face down a few feet from where he was standing. He couldn't help but notice the excessive amount of blood around the body. "Meet Mr. Nicholas Lockett. He's the founder and CEO of Lockett Electronics, which supplies parts for computer processors and motherboards to all the major electronic brands. He has a Master's Degree in engineering from MIT and a net worth of two hundred and fifty million dollars. In other words, dude is loaded." "Wow," responded Marcus. "How'd you find out so much about him so quickly?" "I googled him," responded Logan with a shit eating grin on his face. "Police work at its finest," Marcus joked.

Marcus took a few steps back, reached into his inside jacket pocket, took out a pair of rubber booties and gloves and put them on so he didn't contaminate the scene. He stood there for a few minutes and surveyed the area, taking notes of what the room looked like. Marcus talked to himself out loud. "Nothing looks disturbed. No signs of a struggle. No forced entry. You can't get up here by elevator without a key and a code. He's got a Rolex on his left wrist and his wedding ring is still on." He removed the victim's wallet from his back pants pocket and noted that it contained three one hundred dollar bills. "Doesn't appear to be a robbery."

Have you located a back way into here," he asked Logan? "There's a stairwell that leads to this floor, but there's only one door into the penthouse itself. "You need the same key and a code to get into the stairwell from the lobby" said Logan. "He must have known his killer," they both said at the same time. "Stop reading my mind," joked Logan. "Trust me; the last place that I wanna be is inside that head of yours." "Who found the body," Marcus asked? "Stanley, the concierge. Said he came up to give Mr. Lockett his morning paper and found the door ajar." Marcus looked at Logan with disbelief "people still read newspapers?" "Apparently," responded Logan

Marcus and Logan walked around and approached the body from the feet to get a closer look and to avoid stepping in blood. "Multiple stab wounds to the back" remarked Marcus before they carefully turned him over. "That's a pretty clean cut to the neck, must have been a very large and sharp knife. Looks like the killer was left handed by the direction of the cut," said Marcus. "Yeah, the killer was pissed. Wonder what he did to deserve this," remarked Logan. "Looks like he was also stabbed in the abdomen," Marcus pointed out. "Overkill with the amount of stab wounds. Seems like a crime of passion."

"This wasn't a contract killing," Marcus surmised. "As rich as he is, he must have pissed a few people off on his way to the top, and it's our job to find out whom." "If you're right, the suspect list is gonna be about as long as my dick" joked Logan. Marcus looked up at Logan in disgust "really...you had to go there?" Logan responded with a chuckle.

Just then, another member of Marcus' squad arrived at the scene. Detective Second Grade Anthony Russo, who they refer to as "Big Russ". He's "Mr. Intelligence" who analyzes everything. He's a numbers guy who loves to quote statistics. He is usually way too serious with no sense of humor. Short, round and balding on top. He's been on the police department for thirty-one years and a homicide detective for sixteen of them.

Big Russ walked over to the body without putting on rubber gloves or booties and remarked "this is a bloody mess," in a fake British accent. Marcus and Logan looked at each other with amazement "have you been drinking," Marcus asked? "I had one drink at lunch," replied Detective Russo. "Bullshit," barked Logan, "You look toasted to me and your speech is slurred." "And you're contaminating my scene," said Marcus.

Marcus looked Big Russ in the eyes and said "C'mon man, what are you doing? You need to leave. If

Sarge shows up, you're done." Detective Russo was agitated at their response "I'll go and start the canvass then." Logan shook his head "yeah, that's just what we need. Let the public know you're drunk too. Go home man, I'll tell Sarge you weren't feeling well." Big Russ reluctantly departed.

Marcus and Logan were both surprised. Detective Russo was usually a reliable colleague, but neither one of them ever took the time to really get to know him outside the job. They didn't know the inner struggles he was going through. The mental ghosts that were haunting his life and what was causing the change in his personality. He was slowly turning into the unreliable colleague and was losing the trust of his fellow detectives.

"I assume that the crime scene techs are finished," Marcus asked? "Yep, and I've already requested that the M.E. (Medical Examiner) respond." "Great," said Marcus, "let's take a look around and see what this place tells us." While they were still standing over the body, Logan looks inquisitively at Marcus and says "the other day, I was talking to this guy about a problem I was having with this young lady that we both know and he remarks "familiarity breeds content." "What the hell does that mean?"

Marcus had a puzzled look on his face "I'm not sure but I think that the saying is familiarity breeds contempt, not content." "You can correct me, but you can't tell me what it means," as Logan shook his head. Marcus responded "I've heard that saying before but never really gave it much thought. Did you ask him what it meant?" "Hell no, I didn't want him to know that I didn't know." Agitated now, Logan says "never mind man, forget I asked." Marcus laughed and remarked "oh, your limited vocabulary is my fault?"

They both walked around the penthouse to gather as much evidence as the scene could provide, then departed. On the way out, Stanley the concierge asked "are you guys finished upstairs?" Almost, replied Logan, "as soon as the M.E. takes the body, the officer upstairs will release the scene." Logan looked curiously at the concierge and asked "have you ever heard the term familiarity breeds contempt." Stanley shook his head yes, "but I think its content, not contempt."

Logan looked at Marcus with a smirk on his face. "What do you think it means," asked Logan?" "You have to know someone well to be able to hate them," he replied. Logan shrugged his shoulders as they walked out and said "that shit ain't true, I hate plenty of people that I don't know well." Marcus just shook his head as they left. Once inside his vehicle Marcus squirted some more sanitizer on his hands before driving away.

A.D. White

Chapter Four
Close The Door Behind You

Zero six hundred hours, Monday morning and it was time for roll call. Marcus and Logan were already seated. In walked *Detective Second Class Frank Callahan,* the newest detective to the squad. Detective Callahan had been assigned to the homicide unit for about six months. He was transferred from the Financial Crimes Unit where he specialized in identity theft investigations. Tall, slim, clean shaven with black hair. Had his Master's degree and considered himself an intellectual. Used big words and came across to many as being pretentious. But he wasn't! He was an educated guy that believed that his vocabulary was a reflection of his values and education was his way to success. He looked like a younger version of the Professor on Gilligan's Island, thus they nicknamed him "The Professor."

"Good morning gents, heard you caught a good one yesterday Marcus." "Yeah, it was a great way to spend my Sunday," Marcus sarcastically remarked. "I can see how that might be a precarious predicament" responded Detective Callahan. "Could you speak English when you're in the squad room professor," joked Logan. "Sure, I'll try to use smaller words when I'm around you" was his reply as he sat down. (If you haven't notice by now, all the detectives oozed sarcasm). It was a defense mechanism that briefly took their minds off the seriousness of the job.

Detective Second Class Katelyn Alverez walked into the squad room next. Surprised to see her, Logan jumped up "Hey Al, welcome back," as he opened his arms for a hug. Detective Alverez gave him a "church hug" as Logan tried to move in closer. "Oh, I thought we were past that," Logan joked. "Does that mean you're gonna stop trying to get into my pants," she asked?" Logan sat back down and mumbled "nah, not really." "That's what I thought," replied Detective Alverez as she shook her head in amusement. Despite Logan being a man whore, she had a soft spot for him, but had no intentions on giving him what he really wanted.

Detective Second Grade Katelyn Alverez was nicknamed "Al". She was a hard worker and could never shake the feeling that she had something to prove to the other detectives because she was a female and a minority. She is thirty years old, pretty with long black hair and an hour glass figure. She has been on the department for nine years and in homicide for three of them.

This was Detective Alverez's first day back with the squad. She had been gone awhile due to a past indiscretion. About nine years ago, she made a terrible mistake that almost cost her job. One night In 2006, when she was a patrol officer, Katelyn received a radio run for a burglar alarm at a real estate business in Georgetown. Her father Bennie who was also on the job at the time, happened to be working that night as well, and as he often did, went to assist his baby girl. When Katelyn arrived at the business, the front door was locked but she could hear the alarm sounding. She walked around to the back and noticed that the back door was ajar.

Katelyn and Bennie walked around the business to see if there were obvious signs of anything taken or destroyed. During their search, Bennie opened a closet door that had a safe inside. He turned the handle and much to his amazement, the safe opened. Shocked, Bennie looked inside and discovered that the safe was full of money. He stood there for a moment just staring at the money. Then he grabbed two stacks of bills and stuffed them in the inside pocket of his police jacket just as Katelyn was entering the room. Katelyn stood there in amazement as Bennie looked into her eyes as if to plead for her silence. Katelyn walked out of the room as if she saw nothing.

Months passed and they never spoke of that night until they were contacted by a man named Walter at the police station. Walter explained to Bennie and Katelyn that he worked for the owner of the real estate business and that the owner wanted to meet with them to thank them for protecting his business. It felt like a set up to both of them, but they saw no other way but to attend the meeting.

As they sat, the owner who had introduced himself as Robert said, "I obtained a copy of the police report and saw that the two of you responded to my business a few months ago when the reported burglars broke in. I'd like to thank you for your service." They both nodded. "By the way, I noticed that you have the same last name, are you two related?" "Yes," answered Bennie "this is my daughter." "You must be very proud," responded Robert. Bennie nodded once more. "Well, I never like to beat around the bush so I'm going to get straight to the point."

"In addition to the alarm, I have video surveillance of the premises and there's something that I want you to see." Robert picked up the remote control on his desk and turned on the flat screen television on the wall. The video clearly showed Bennie opening the safe, removing two stacks of money and placing it into his pockets. "The clarity is remarkable, wouldn't you agree," asked Robert? Bennie sighed, "yeah, it's pretty good." The video also captured Katelyn standing there watching Bennie, then Robert cut if off.

Robert leaned back in his chair "officers, we have a problem. Twenty thousand dollars was missing from my safe and the police report doesn't mention it. Bennie leaned forward, "listen, I know what I did was wrong. I still have most of the money and I can give it back to you." "It's not about the money," Robert responded. "It's about trust. We trust the officers in this city to do the right thing and I'm sure that most of them do, but apparently you're the exception to that rule."

Bennie and Katelyn sat there in stunned silence. "Let my daughter leave, she has nothing to do with this. We can discuss how I can pay you back," said Bennie. "I beg to differ," Robert responded. "She saw what you did and that makes her part of it. You involved your daughter, but I have a solution."

They both looked at Robert with baited breath. "Keep the money. Think of it as a contribution" he said. "A contribution to what," Bennie asked. "A contribution for your cooperation," Robert responded. "What do I have to do" Bennie inquired? "Not I, we. You're not in this by yourself," responded Robert.

"As much as you would like for this not to involve your daughter, it does. But you don't have to do anything for it...right now! There may come a time when I need a favor and you have been paid in advance for that favor. It's up to you. You can agree to be my friends or Internal Affairs can view the tape. Your choice, but you don't have a lot of time to decide. I'm gonna need to know right now how you want me to handle this."

"You want nothing right now," Bennie asked? "That's correct; you can walk out of here with a clean conscious. The money's yours. I may or may not need something from you in the future," said Robert. Bennie and Katelyn looked into Robert's cold, dark eyes and agreed to his terms. They had just made a deal with the devil! Bennie retired from the police department two months later and Katelyn didn't receive nor want any of the money that her father took.

Eight years later when it came time to repay the favor to Robert, Katelyn chose to report these facts to her lieutenant and then to Internal Affairs, rather than to submit to blackmail. Detective Alverez was sent to an administrative trial board, which convened to determine her fate. Much to everyone's surprise, the trial board took into consideration her coming forward on her own and her exemplary record. Not to mention the fact that her father took the money, leaving her with an unbearable choice to make. She received a thirty day suspension without pay. The owner of the money chose not to cooperate with the police and her father was not prosecuted.

Detective Sergeant Ulysses Gant entered the room to conduct roll call. He was the squad sergeant. They referred to him as Sergeant U or just Sarge. Sergeant U was a thirty year veteran of the police department and a former homicide detective. He was short, round and sarcastic. "Rose," he barked. "Here Sarge" replied Marcus. "Steele." Logan just looked at Sarge and didn't respond. Sergeant U looked directly at Logan and again barked "Steele". "You're looking right at me Sarge, you know I'm here" replied Logan. Sergeant U again barked "Steele". "Here Sarge," Logan finally replied. Sergeant U looked at Detective Steele and said "now that wasn't so hard, was it?"

Steele mumbled something that was unintelligible to everyone else. "Yo mama," replied Sergeant U as he continued "Detective Russo". Silence. "Anybody seen Russo," he asked? "Not since yesterday at the crime scene," responded Marcus. "He was a little under the weather," added Logan. The sergeant responded with a smirk on his face. "Callahan" continued the sergeant. "Present, sergeant," he replied. "And last but not least, Alverez" said Sergeant U. She responded with her usual "aqui".

Lieutenant O'Malley entered the squad room. "Okay ladies; brief me on yesterday's scene." Marcus stood up, "the victim's name was Nicholas Lockett. He's the founder and CEO of Lockett Electronics, which supplies parts for computer processors and motherboards to all the major electronic brands. Educated at MIT and had a net worth of around a couple hundred million dollars."

"Okay" responded the Lieutenant. "I've heard of him. Sort of an asshole. Part of his charm was his business sense and ruthlessness." Everyone seemed impressed with the lieutenant's knowledge of the victim, but as usual, Detective Steele had something smart to say. "Oh, you must watch TMZ, Lieu." Lieutenant O'Malley just looked at Detective Steele unimpressed, then turned his attention to Sergeant U. "Where's Detective Russo?" "Don't know Lieu, but I'll find out" he replied. "Have him come see me as soon as he gets in." "Yes sir," replied Sergeant U.

Lieutenant O'Malley turned his attention back to Marcus. "Okay, what else you got?" "The vic was stabbed multiple times, but it looks like the kill shot was a slice to his jugular. The cut pattern went from the killer's left to the right, so if they were facing each other, the killer had to be left handed" continued Marcus. "The crime techs found a partial print that they're still analyzing. No signs of forced entry and nothing was missing. It appears that he knew his killer. He was married, no kids. I'm going to his place of business and see what I can find out from his employees." "Good job Marcus, keep me informed. Also, in the press release just mention that the manner of death was by stabbing. Don't mention where or how many times he was stabbed. Let's play this one close to the vest" said the lieutenant as he turned his back and walked toward his office.

"Alverez, in my office" he barked as he walked out. Alverez got up and followed him into his office. "Close the door behind you" he instructed her. "Yes sir Lieu," she replied as she stood in front of his desk.

"Have a seat Alverez. First of all, welcome back" "Thank you sir, I'm happy to be back," she replied.

"Listen, I'm not going to sugar coat this. You fucked up, but you took responsibility for your actions and that's the only reason that I gave my blessing for you to remain in Homicide. But understand this, there can be no other slip ups. Everything that you do has to be by the numbers. You gotta cross your T's and dot your I's. Consider yourself on probation for the next year and if you want to be in Homicide, you have to be the example, not an example. Do you understand what I'm saying?" She was a little confused by that last sentence, but she replied "Yes sir". "You're a damn good detective, but I've gotta be able to trust you if you're gonna remain in this unit." Lieutenant O'Malley then started looking at papers on his desk and without looking up he said "close the door behind you." Detective Alverez stood up and walked out.

Just as she was exiting, Detective Russo was entering. "You wanted to see me Lieu?" Still rummaging through the papers on his desk "Have a seat Russo." "Yes sir Lieu, what's this about" he asked. Lieutenant O'Malley stopped, looked up and said "it's about you and your alcohol problem." "Who told you that Lieu" was Detective Russo's reply. Now, Lieutenant O'Malley was rarely in a good mood and Detective Russo's response didn't help. "Do you think that I'm a fucking idiot Russo" asked the Lieutenant? "No sir," replied Detective Russo.

"You've been coming in here for months smelling like a fucking brewery and this morning is not the first time that you've been late for roll call." Detective Russo lowered his head in embarrassment. "Right now, you are a liability to this unit and to the department. I'm putting you on sick leave for the next week. Get yourself some help. If you gotta start going to AA, then do that. Whatever avenue you have to pursue to get your shit together, do it. By the time you report back here next Monday, I'd better see a change in you. Be on time and sober or put your retirement papers in. Those are your only two choices!" Lieutenant O'Malley put his head back down and started rummaging through his papers again and said "CLOSE THE DOOR BEHIND YOU."

Chapter Five
Blurred Lines

To say that Detective Anthony Russo had some hard decisions to make would be an understatement. He had been on the department for thirty-one years and was eligible to retire any time he wanted. The problem was that he had made the department his life. He gave everything that he had to the job. He was married to it. If or better yet, when he retired he was afraid that it would be a lonely existence. Some people look forward to retirement while others fear it.

He was a good detective but an absent husband. One day he came home and his wife was gone, along with all their furniture. He walked into the house, and for a brief moment, thought he had wandered into the wrong place. He called out to Patty, but all he heard was his own echo. All she left him was a bottle of whiskey in the cupboard. That's when alcohol became his best friend and the beginning to his end.

He always found a reason to drink and then after a while, he didn't need a reason. It was part of his lonely nights, but of lately, it had become part of his days also. In the past he never drank before coming to work. Now he didn't know where his nights ended and his days began. The lines were blurred. He was officially a drunk and on the road to destruction.

The day that Lieutenant O'Malley gave him an ultimatum, Big Russ went home and repeated his daily ritual. A ritual that no one else knew about. He sat in his living room recliner with the end table on his right. On that table, he'd placed a bottle of whiskey and a shot glass. Next to the shot glass he placed his old revolver that he carried in his rookie years.   Before the department went to semi-automatic handguns.

He would drink shot after shot, getting his nerve up. The nerve to place one bullet in the cylinder of the revolver, spin and close it. He would place the gun to his head and pull the trigger. Russian Roulette. He had a one in six chance that this would be his last day. Either he would hear the click of the empty chamber or he would hear nothing at all as the bullet entered his skull.

Chapter Six
Just an Observation

The next day Lieutenant O'Malley assembled the squad for another update on the case. "Marcus, where are we at on this," he asked? "Well Lieu, we know the victim is married, very wealthy and the CEO of a major electronics company. We know that he owns the penthouse that he was murdered at and it appears that his wife did not stay there at all." "Why do you say that" asked Sergeant U? "The place screamed bachelor's pad. no woman's clothes in the closet. No pictures of the wife anywhere. The décor itself lacked a woman's touch. He took the term Man Cave to a whole different level," replied Marcus.

Marcus continued, "access to the penthouse is restricted. There is one elevator that is exclusively used to access the penthouse. You need a key to call the elevator; once inside, there is a code that has to be entered into a keypad to go the penthouse. Only the victim and the concierge have the code." "Callahan, check with the building manager and find out who the concierges were for the twenty-four hour period before the victim was found and how many total concierges are employed there." "Copy, Lieu" responded Detective Callahan.

"According to the M.E., the victim's throat was cut. He was stabbed once in the abdomen and stabbed ten times in the back after he fell to the floor. It only took him a couple of minutes to die from the neck wound. This was personal, he knew his killer," said Marcus. I think Al would be just the right person to interview his wife. She has a knack for getting information out of people," Marcus said as he looked to the Lieutenant for his approval. The lieutenant nodded in agreement. "People like to share with me, what can I say," joked Detective Alverez.

"Detective Steele, look into his finances. Find out what secrets he's been hiding," said the lieutenant. "What makes you think that he had secrets," Logan asked? Marcus grinned "everybody's got secrets." "Even you," whispered Logan? Marcus ignored that remark as his grin disappeared. "I'll interview his employees and find out what kind of man he really was," Marcus continued. "This is good for starters and maybe it will help us find out who had the most to gain from his death. Who has a motive to kill him? Did he have a will, life insurance? Who gains control of his company now that he's gone? When we find out those answers, we'll be closer to finding the killer," said Marcus. "Okay ladies," said Sergeant U, "that's the game plan for today. We'll update the case tomorrow in roll call."

Logan approached Marcus "I've got a contact at the Department of Consumer and Regulatory Affairs who can tell me if there are any co-owners on file for Lockett

Electronics. Wanna ride," he asked. Nah, I've gotta take care of something, then I'll go to his job. I might be a little bit," Marcus said with a distant look on his face. "Alright," said Logan while turning to Detective Callahan. "Come on professor; let's take a ride. I can school you a little bit," he said with a grin. The two walked out to Logan's unmarked cruiser.

"So your partner ditched you today," Callahan said, real inquisitive like? "Nah, he's got something mysterious to take care of." "I noticed that he gets lost every now and then," said Callahan as he raised an eyebrow. "Maybe he's got a woman on the side," he continued. Logan looked at him angrily, "Marcus wouldn't do no shit like that. He and his wife Gina have a solid marriage," said Logan. Callahan threw his hands up in the air, "alright, my thoughts are inconsequential in this matter." Logan shook his head as they got into the car.

Sensing that Logan was irritated, Callahan looked at him and said "listen, I'm not suggesting any duplicity on your partner's behalf. I was just making an observation. A peripheral view from an outsider is all it was." Logan ignored him as he started the car, turned on the car radio, adjusted the volume up and drove off. When they arrived downtown and got out of the car, a street type fellow approached Logan. "Steele, how ya doing my brother," he asked. "Well if it ain't Freddie the Fact Finder," Logan said with a laugh. Logan turned to

Callahan and said "Freddie's an old C.I. (confidential informant) of mine from my days in narcotics. Freddie's always got his ears to the street."

Freddie smiled, "you know me Steele. I'm a seller of inflammation." "Do you mean information," Logan asked Freddie with a big grin? "You know exactly what I mean. I can find out what ever you need me to find out about and as always, I will need to be complicated for my services."

Logan laughed, "you know that I will compensate you for any good info you've got. If it helps me solve a case, you get paid." Callahan leaned over to Logan and jokingly asked "is English his second language?" Freddie overheard Callahan and asked, "who's this bama? I know he ain't the popo." "This is Detective Frank Callahan. He's my partner for the day," replied Logan. Freddie looked Callahan up and down and said "he looks like the professor from Gilligan's Island." Logan chuckled and said, "you think?"

"I ain't seen you in a while Steele. I heard you weren't in narcotics no more though. You the murder police now, huh Steele." "Yeah Freddie," he replied. "I'm just like George Jefferson, moving on up." "Okay, I see you big pimpin. You know I still got you," Freddie said. "Okay Freddie," said Callahan "since you know so much, there was a homicide in a high rise on Mass. Avenue. Can you find out anything about that?" Logan interrupted, "Freddie knows the street, but I don't think he knows about the high rise life." "Oh, now you trying to play me, huh Steele? Haven't I've always been informative?" "Yes you have, but this guy Nicholas Lockett, he runs in different circles Freddie."

"Okay Steele, I'll take that as a challenge. You got the same number?" "Yep, it's the same, 555-0964." "I'll be in touch," said Freddie. He then looked at Detective Callahan and said "this gump here probably still got a pager. You want me to beep you?" Callahan laughed and said, "no superfluous communication between us will be necessary Freddie." Easily insulted, Freddie said, "I'll take that as a no" and started to walk away.

He then stopped and walked over to Detective Steele and whispered "Yo Steele, do me a solid. I'm a little short, so can I get an advance on the info that I'm gonna have for you?" "Alright Freddie, but this ain't charity. I'm gonna need a return on my money," said Steele as he reached into his pocket and gave Freddie two twenty dollar bills. Freddie replied, "I got you Steele. You know me," as he smiled and walked away.

They proceeded into the building of Consumer and Regulatory Affairs. "That guys a real character, I need a translator to understand his ass," said Detective Callahan. "He's a funny dude; he murders the English language but once you figure out what he's saying, he always has good info," replied Logan. "We'll see if he can provide any info on this case. It doesn't hurt to ask.

Speaking of info, I know this chick named Felicia that works here. She can give us some info on Nicholas Lockett's business.

They took the elevator to the fifth floor, turned left and went through the double glass doors. There was a very attractive woman at the desk. Short black curly hair, pretty face, abundantly chested and about thirty years old. She was looking down, reading something. "Hey beautiful," said Logan. She looked up "uumh, Logan Steele," she said with a wary smirk on her face.

"You must need something," she said as she rolled her eyes. "I need you," he responded. "Cut the crap Logan, as soon as you get what you want, a sista never hears from you again. That's your M.O. Seeing that you're standing right in front of me now, means that you want something." Logan sighed heavily. "Look Felicia, I've just been really busy. The job keeps crazy hours and I know that you need a man that can dedicate more time to you than I'm able to give." Felicia tilted her head to the left, placed her chin in her hand and said "really", then yawned. Logan started off "listen Boo" and Felicia mumbled under her breath "oh now I'm Boo." "Felicia, I'm really sorry that I haven't been in touch; how about I take you to dinner this weekend," he asked? "I'll think about it" she replied again with that same smirk. "What can I help you with Detective?"

"I need some inflammation." Steele and Callahan burst into laughter, but seeing that this was an inside joke, Felicia didn't share their amusement. She just stared at him until he gained his composure. "I'm sorry Felicia, inside joke. I need some information on a business called Lockett Electronics. I need to know who all the owners and major players are for the business and can you tell me if they're current with all their taxes?" "Is that all you need Logan" she asked? "If you sprinkle that with a little forgiveness too, that would be nice" was his reply. "Who's your friend" she asked. "Oh, this is Detective Frank Callahan, my partner for the day." "Lucky him" she mumbled. Logan just shook his head as he held back a devilish grin.

She turned to her computer screen and started typing. After a few minutes she turned back to Logan "the majority owner is Nicholas Lockett. He owns 51%. The minority owner is Brandon Lockett. He owns the remaining 49% and they are current and up to date with all taxes." "Thank you Felicia, I really appreciate it. Can I call you later?" With hesitation, she responded "I guess." Logan leaned over the desk and kissed her on the cheek "you smell good, what are you wearing" he asked. She looked deep into Logan's eyes and responded "Coochie." Logan laughed out loud and said "I want some of that." "Maybe, if you act right," was her reply. Logan and Callahan then walked away.

As he turned the corner, Logan looked back and made eye contact with Felicia as she watched him walk away. As they got into the elevator, Callahan said to

Logan "I think she likes you." Logan sarcastically replied, "you think?" "Just an observation" responded Callahan as the elevator door closed.

Chapter Seven
It's True What They Say

After Marcus finished his errand, he drove to Lockett Electronics on Wisconsin Avenue, in Northwest D.C. Parking was unbearable in that part of the city during that time of day. Marcus parked his unmarked police car at the corner and placed his strobe light on the dash to avoid being ticketed. As he exited his vehicle, he stopped and gathered the city view. The concrete jungle with tall buildings all around. He took a deep breath and breathed in the city air. Something would make most people choke, but Marcus loved the smell of the city. Hundreds of cars coming and going, horns beeping, people walking about on their lunch breaks or shopping at stores. Every so often a police car or ambulance would speed by with their sirens screaming.

"I love this city," Marcus said to himself as he reached into his jacket pocket and removed his hand sanitizer to clean his hands before walking into the entrance of Lockett Electronics. Marcus approached the receptionist and couldn't help but notice that the young lady sitting behind the desk was quite stunning. She appeared to be in her late twenties, blonde hair and blue eyes. A real looker! He showed her his police ID "afternoon ma'am. I'm Detective Rose from the D.C. Police Department and I need to talk to the person in charge." The receptionist looked Marcus up and down, then smiled. "That would be Mr. Lockett, I'll give him a call," she responded. Marcus' left brow raised, surprised that there was another Mr. Lockett. She picked up the phone and dialed his number. "Mr. Lockett, there's a detective here that would like to speak with you sir. Yes sir, I'll show him the way."

She stood up, exposing her perfect figure and pointed down the hall "go down this hallway to the elevator. Take the elevator to the third floor. That will take you to the offices. Go through the double glass doors, then you'll go through an open area with desks and cubicles on your left. Mr. Lockett's office is the last door on the right." "Thanks" replied Marcus, "and your name is," he asked? "My name is Ashley," she said with a smile.

Marcus took the elevator to the third floor and proceeded through the double doors. As he walked through the open area, he saw about a dozen people working at their cubicles. All of which stared at him as he walked to the end of the hall. As he approached the office, a well groomed gentleman greeted him at the door. He extended his hand, "Hi, I'm Brandon Lockett. You must be here about my brother." Marcus shook his hand "yes sir, my name is Detective Marcus Rose and I'm investigating...he paused for a split second, the death of your brother." "You mean the murder of my brother detective?" "Yes, to put it bluntly," Marcus responded.

"Have a seat detective. How can I help you?" Marcus sat down as Brandon Lockett walked behind his large mahogany desk and sat. His office was luxurious. Large windows behind him that looked out onto Wisconsin Avenue. Wooden built-in bookshelves. Large comfortable overstuffed leather chair that matched the mahogany desk. A far cry from where Marcus sat in the Homicide office.

"Mr. Lockett, do you have any idea who would have done this to your brother," Marcus asked? Brandon Lockett looked at Marcus with hesitation "the list is long detective." "You don't say," replied Marcus. "My brother Nicholas was kinda ruthless. I handled the operational aspect of the business. Developing the software and that sort of thing. He handled the money side of the company. Pitching our product to the companies and persuading them to buy our product."

"Every time we won a contract with one of the major carriers or stores, he made another enemy. Our competitors felt like we were taking too much money out of their pockets and in a way, I guess we were. But that's business. You know, it's true what they say." "What's that," Marcus questioned. "The love of money. It will make people act out of character." Marcus shook his head in disagreement, "actually, it will show a man's true character," Marcus retorted. Brandon Lockett reluctantly nodded his head in agreement.

After viewing the original crime scene, Marcus had a feeling that Nicholas Lockett's murder was personal, not business. Although any scenario was possible at this point and he was open to all theories. "Do you think that any of his business rivals would want him dead," asked Marcus? "Only one comes to mind" replied Brandon. "Diedrick Becker. A German business man who attempted a hostile takeover of our company. As usual, Nicholas was one step ahead of everyone else and saw it coming. Diedrick is a very proud man and his attempt at a takeover failed miserably. I think that he would be capable of killing my brother or at least paying someone to do it. I'll have my brother's personal assistant give you Diedrick's contact information." Marcus saw this as a substantial lead and was very appreciative.

"Tell me about your brother's personal life. I know that he was married, but was he seeing anyone else?" Brandon Lockett leaned back in his chair "that list was long also. Let's just say that my brother had an insatiable appetite." "Do you know who your brother was seeing," Marcus asked? "He talked about his conquests, but he didn't mention many names. The only name that I remember from his past is Angelika. I guess that I remember that one because it's such a pretty name." "Yeah, it is," replied Marcus, "I think it means Angel. Can you tell me anything about her and most of all do you know how I can get in touch with her," asked Marcus? "I only know that she was married," replied Brandon. "Presently, he was seeing his personal assistant Nicole. He never admitted it, but they are very close and knowing my brother, I'd be shocked if they weren't screwing." "I'll need her information" said Marcus. "That's easy Detective. She sits outside of Nicholas' office, right next door."

What was your relationship like with your brother," Marcus inquired? "Well truthfully," Brandon started to say. (Marcus thought to himself that every time someone starts a sentence with "well truthfully" there's gonna be a lie somewhere in that story). Brandon continued, "We didn't always get along but we made a great team." "What did you guys disagree on," Marcus asked? "His lifestyle. My brother worked hard and he played hard." "Do tell," Marcus responded. "Frankly, I had a problem with him screwing around on his wife and screwing other people's wives. It's messy and eventually creates a conflict of interest. Not to mention the fact that he's married to a wonderful woman. He had it all but was never satisfied." "Did the two of you have any business disagreements," Marcus questioned him. "No, he did his job well which made us a lot of money and I had no problem with that." "Did you know about the penthouse that he kept in the city," Marcus asked. "I had no idea that he had that place, but that was just like Nicolas...keeping secrets," said Brandon.

Marcus stood up and extended his hand "Thank you for your time Mr. Lockett. Do you think that you can provide me Diedrick Becker's information as well as his personal assistants?" "Sure detective." Brandon Lockett picked up the phone and pressed the intercom "Nicole, please come to my office."

Thirty seconds later a tall slim blonde woman with pretty blue eyes walked into the office "yes Mr. Lockett." "Detective, this is my brother's personal assistant Nicole." Marcus nodded to her and she nodded back. Marcus couldn't help but notice that she seemed very solemn. "Please provide Detective Rose with Diedrick Becker's contact information and assist him with anything else he needs pertaining to my brother." Marcus handed her his business card. "Can you email that to me as well as a number that I can reach you at" Marcus asked? "Yes sir" she replied as she walked out of the office.

"She seems to be taking your brother's death very hard." Marcus started walking towards the door. He then stopped, turned around and asked "with your brother gone, who inherits his share of the company?" "I do," Brandon responded with a matter of fact look on his face. "You be careful Mr. Lockett. A lot of people want what you have and apparently they will do anything to get it." Brandon sat back down "thanks for your concern, but I'll be okay."

You know it's true what they say detective." Marcus looked at him inquisitively and said "enlighten me." "Money is power and I'll be just fine," he replied.

Marcus smiled "you know what else they say?" "What's that detective," Brandon inquired? "Those who own much, have much to fear." Marcus wondered why this seemed like a cat and mouse game. Brandon Lockett was feeding him information, little by little. "If you were me, who else would you talk to about your brother?" Brandon thought to himself "If I was you, I'd kill myself." Then he smiled and replied "I'd probably talk to Nicholas' driver Stephan Richardson." "Nicholas had a driver" Marcus asked as he began to be annoyed by Brandon's little game?

"Yes. You know how hard it is to find parking around the city. His driver took him everywhere!" Marcus really wasn't a violent man, but at this point he had an overwhelming desire to smack the shit out of Brandon. But being the mature law enforcement professional that he was, he suppressed that feeling. "Would it be possible to get his contact information also," Marcus asked? "Certainly Detective. I'll have Nicole email you that information too."

Before I leave, do you have any questions for me" said Marcus? Brandon shook his head yes "do you know how the killer got the key and code to get to the penthouse?" "No sir, still trying to figure that one out" said Marcus as he left the office. Before leaving the building, Marcus stopped at the bathroom to wash his hands once more.

A.D. White

Chapter Eight
Nicholas Lockett

Nicholas Lockett was a multifaceted man. Tall, slim and good looking. Short black hair with a tanned body. Not only smart, but clever too. But his most admirable quality was his charisma. He was so charming that he could sell ice to an Eskimo. He rarely heard the word no and when he did, he didn't take it well; Nicholas also had a dark side. He was capable of almost anything!

There's a fine line between confidence and arrogance and Nicholas could be both. He would show the side that he wanted people to see. If you found him to be arrogant, it's because he wanted you to see him that way. He saw arrogance and confidence as a manipulation tool and used each to get his desired results.

The Lockett brothers grew up in Philadelphia, Pennsylvania. They came from a well to do family and much was expected of he and his younger brother Brandon. Brandon graduated from Columbia University in Manhattan, New York. He had a degree in Computer Science. While in college, Brandon got mixed up in a cheating scheme, where he hacked into the colleges administrative computers and changed grades for a fee. I guess you could say that it was the first business he ever owned. His father donated money to the college and Brandon was allowed to graduate.

Their father was an attorney who owned his own law firm and became rich defending wealthy criminals. The Lockett brothers characters were molded by watching their father defend guilty people for profit. His father would always say that guilty people need lawyers and guilty rich people need lawyers even more. His bottom line was getting paid. True innocence or guilt never entered into the equation.

Nicholas and Brandon looked up to their father and were products of their environment. They were bread to be successful by any means necessary. To most of us a half truth is a whole lie, but not to the Lockett boys. To them a half-truth was an end to a means. Say what you have to, to get whatever you need. Lie, cheat or steal if you have to. Nice guys finish last! They learned to manipulate and shave the truth as long as their objective was obtained in the end.

Nicholas met his wife Yvette in college. She was bright and attractive but lacked the aggressiveness to become successful in the world of finance. Or should I say, she lacked the ruthlessness. Tall, slim with blonde hair and blue eyes. She had been totally swept off her feet by Nicholas. He charmed the pants right off her (so to speak). They married right after college and she happily shared in his success. Yvette worked for a little while but when the Lockett brothers decided to open up their business in D.C., at Nicholas' request, she became a full time wife. She was his trophy wife who attended elaborate events on his arm. It always helps to be seen with a pretty woman and Yvette was a real looker. Yvette really loved Nicholas and in the beginning wanted to believe anything that he told her. She chose to see the good in him and turned a blind eye to his faults. But that couldn't last forever! Just because she was blonde and pretty didn't mean that she was stupid!

Nicholas had affairs with other women and in the beginning he did his best to shield Yvette from finding out about his extracurricular activities. But just like most people, when you get away with something for so long, they become careless and sometimes they just care less. Yvette had one friend in the world. That one girlfriend that she trusted and could tell anything to. Being best friends meant that she allowed this woman into her home and into both their lives.

Her friend was savvy with computers and needed a better job. Being the friend that she was, Yvette talked to Nicholas about her working at his company. You know that old theory, instead of giving someone a meal you teach them how to fish so that they can acquire their own meal. Seemed like a good idea at the time.

Nicholas was more than happy to grant her wish. Her friend was an excellent employee and went on to work there for many years. Being the man that he was,

Nicholas eventually started seeing Yvette's friend in a different light. As if one day she suddenly became attractive.

Every time that Nicholas crossed paths with her they would exchange smiles. If he was talking to one person and she was in the room he would constantly glance her way. He couldn't keep his eyes off of her. She noticed his glances and was intrigued by his interest in her. They were forbidden fruit to each other which only intensified their growing lust. Surely he wouldn't have an affair with his wife's best friend, would he?

Nicholas summoned her to his office one day. She was understandably nervous, wondering what in the world he wanted. She stopped at his open door and knocked. "Please, come in," as he looked up at the door with a smile. "I was told to come and see you." "Yes, come in and have a seat. He watched her intently as she sat. Her short black skirt clinged to her body and exposed her thighs as she sat and crossed her legs.

"I'm thinking about hiring a personal assistant. You've been here for a while and have been doing a great job. Your supervisor has nothing but good things to say about your work. This is a chance for advancement in the company and a substantial pay raise. "Really," she said as she uncrossed her legs and sat up straight in her chair. "What does the job entail and how much does it pay," she inquired. Nicholas laughed "straight to the point. I like that. The job would require you to attend to my needs" he said with a devilish grin.

You would plan my day, schedule my appointments, answer my office phone and take care of my personal needs." "Your personal needs? I'm not sure I know what you mean by that," she replied. "Nicole, my personal needs may change from day to day. One day it could be listening to me vent. Another day it could be getting my lunch or dinner; I work crazy hours sometimes. The next day I may need you to massage my neck. This is a very hands on *position*! I'll need you to anticipate my needs and act accordingly."

Nicole smiled, "I believe I understand what you want. How much does this...position pay," she asked again. "What's your salary now," Nicholas asked? "Seventy thousand dollars," she replied. "I'll double that, but remember this is a fluid position and requires you to anticipate my needs." "What about Yvette," she asked? Nicholas flashed his signature devilish grin "you let me worry about Yvette, this is business," he replied. Nicole shook her head yes "I'm interested in this...position."

Nicholas looked into her eyes and said, "okay, you're hired." Nicole flashed a sensual smile, stood up and straightened her dress. Then she turned around and closed the office door with her on the inside. As she walked toward Nicholas she said, "I'd like to make the right impression on my first day in my new position" as she unbuttoned her blouse. Nicholas flashed that devilish grin once more, "call me crazy, but I think you're gonna work out fine."

Chapter Nine
Broken

For some reason the day's events wore Marcus down. It was probably the accumulation of his past few cases. It's only a matter of time before everyone has to do some soul searching. To look at yourself in the mirror and determine if you're fulfilling your prophecy. That's if you've figured out and come to terms with what your prophecy is.

His personality was pretty steady. He wasn't a bubbly person, but he wasn't a pessimist either. Marcus was somewhere in the middle most of the time and always tried to think positive. Being a cop for all these years takes a toll on you. His job forced him to see the worst that society had to offer. Over the years Marcus had seen it all. He saw his share of heroic cops but he also saw his share of dirty ones too. Unfortunately, a few bad apples can skew the landscape and overshadow the accomplishments of the good ones. And right now, the news was saturated by pictures and videos of the allegedly corrupt cops which made it hard on everyone else. Then there's the accumulative factor of seeing death, destruction and disappointment throughout the years on the job.

Marcus went home, changed out of his suit and tie and took a shower. It was his custom to wash off the stink of crime before interacting with his family. He rarely took his job home by discussing his cases with Gina. He made a conscious choice to keep his job and home separate. He did not want to bring that dark cloud into his home because his home was his sanctuary and he didn't want that filth there.

Marcus went to his man cave, closed the door, turned on some music and reflected on the past. He thought about all the lives he had touched. All the people he had crossed paths with through the job. Thought about the co-workers and friends that he no longer kept in touch with. He wondered if these last twenty something years on the job were all in vain or if he had made a difference in anyone's life. He thought about the cops that he knew when he was a young officer. The ones that started out good but somehow lost their way. Some were fired, some resigned. He wondered how he'd made it all these years unscathed. We all have done some stupid shit when we were younger. Sometimes you get a pass and have the opportunity to learn from your mistakes. Other times you pay for them immediately and that changes the direction of the rest of your life.

He thought about the men and women in blue that turned to alcohol for their outlet. They drank to dull the pain of what they saw day to day. People living in poverty. Dead bodies lying in the street for no good reason. Domestic violence. Robberies, burglaries, suicides. The worst that society has to offer, day after day, year after year, over and over again. What Marcus didn't realize is that he wasn't unscathed. He bore the same scars that his colleagues did.

All these years later, he still remembered the first homicide that he responded to as a rookie officer. The first time that he had to tell a family that their loved one was dead. He will never forget the first deceased child that saw. You tuck it away in the recesses of your mind because that's the only way you can move forward, but it's still there.

Everyone handled it differently, but they were all broken in some kind of way. His career affected his mind and the way he thought about certain situations. He bore the unmistakable traits of a cop. For example, most people pull straight into parking spots. Marcus always backed into parking spots to be able to leave in a hurry if he had to. When he went out to dinner with Gina, he preferred to sit with his back against the wall so that he could see everyone coming and going.

Out in public, he watched people, always looking for the next fool that was going to shoot up a mall or business. He was all too aware of life's dangers and the evil that men do. Even though he wasn't a skeptic, he trusted very few people. A hazard of the job you could say. How you handled these stresses made the difference in determining your path. You had to decide if your life experiences were going to be a destructive force or a motivating one.

Marcus turned to God a long time ago. He wasn't what you'd call a religious man, but he was spiritual. He attended church and went to bible study regularly at an early age. His mother and grandmother saw to that. This is where his foundation was established. He didn't have a choice until he became an adult. Even though he wasn't in church every Sunday now, his faith was still with him. His values and principles had been ingrained in him long ago. That and a strong family structure helped Marcus survive the trying times in his life.

No, he didn't make the right decisions all the time and he was painfully aware that he was not a perfect man. But Marcus had a quiet strength to him. He was honest and had integrity. All his experiences over the years molded him into the man that he was today. Mature and confident. He could relate to what others were going through because he lived it also. You know the scripture: if any of you are without sin, cast the first stone. Well Marcus wasn't throwing any stones.

But for some reason, God smiled upon him. He wasn't sure why. Why some people's lives had crumbled and his had strengthened. Knowing that we are all capable of stumbling and falling at any moment, kept him humble. And being humble was his best quality. Being humble didn't mean that he couldn't be strong and confident. It meant that he didn't look down on others when they made mistakes. He had compassion.

While going through this self-evaluation process, Marcus came to the conclusion that being a police officer was his calling. No, this job wasn't for everyone, but this is what he was meant to do. Despite the bad apples, being a police officer made a difference in society. Even if he didn't hear thank you or receive awards, being a police officer in D.C. meant something. He was giving back to the city that he grew up in. If you could survive here, you could survive anywhere. God smiles upon the men and women who protect others with honesty and integrity and do not put themselves above the law. Marcus was the epitome of that description.

A.D. White

Chapter Ten
Plausible Deniability

Detective Katelyn Alverez went to Nicholas Lockett's residence to interview his wife Yvette. She drove up to their brick mansion, tucked away behind large oak trees and a wrought iron fence in the upper Northwest section of D.C. near Embassy row. She stopped at the gate and pressed the intercom. "Can I help you" the female voice from the intercom asked? "Yes ma'am, my name is Detective Katelyn Alverez from the D.C. Police Department and I'm here to speak with Mrs. Yvette Lockett. She heard a buzzing sound and the large wrought iron gate opened inward. She drove through the gate and into a circular driveway as the gate closed behind her.

Detective Alverez was dressed moderately, in gray pants suit with a white blouse. After exiting her vehicle, she straightened her suit jacket and brushed a piece of lint off her sleeve. This is what the good life looks like huh, she thought to herself. She walked up the stairs and rang the doorbell. After a few seconds, the door opened and she was greeted by the maid. "Hi Detective, come in. Ms. Lockett is waiting for you in the parlor," as she pointed up the circular stairs to the second floor landing. Alverez walked up the stairs and was greeted by this tall blonde bombshell. She wasn't quite what

Alverez expected to see. "Hi officer, I'm Yvette Lockett. I've been expecting you."

"That's Detective ma'am, Detective Alverez" as she extended her hand. "Call me Yvette" she said as they shook hands. Alverez continued "I'm sorry for your loss Yvette, but I have a few questions that I need to ask you." "Anything that you need Detective, I will help in any way that I can. Let's go into the parlor and have a seat." They walked into the parlor and sat. "Is there anyone that comes to mind that might want to harm your husband," Alverez asked? "No, I don't know much about his business dealings" she responded. "What about in his personal life" Alverez asked? "No" she responded.

"I really hate to be blunt, but in cases such as this, there are a lot of hard questions that need to be asked," Alverez informed her. "I understand Detective, ask what you may," replied Yvette. "Were you and your husband faithful to each other?" Yvette paused for a second "I suspect that my husband has had his share of indiscretions. He was very friendly, to put it lightly. There was something about Nicholas. He always had a way of attracting strays." "And how did that make you feel," Alverez asked. Oh, this bitch is Dr. Phil, Yvette thought to herself. "I wasn't happy about it but it really didn't affect anything that went on inside this house. I didn't know about his little bachelor's pad. I'm sure that's where he did all his dirt and as long as he didn't bring his strumpets in this house, I could pretend that it didn't happen. You know, plausible deniability in a way. If I don't see it, it didn't happen."

"Wow…okay. So his extra-curricular activities didn't anger you," Alverez asked? "Not enough to kill him, if that's what you're asking Detective." "Do you know who he was seeing and if they had any reason to harm him," Alverez further inquired? "I assume that he was screwing my ex-best friend who also happens to be his personal assistant Nicole. She seemed to worship the ground that he walked upon," Yvette said with a little more distain.

"You seem surprised Detective," Yvette went on to say. "Actually I am, Mrs. Lockett. I don't think that I would feel the same way if I were married and my husband was screwing around on me" said Alverez. Yvette looked as if she was holding back a smirk, "I have a unique situation Detective. Look around. No matter what he does, I'm not letting anyone of those bitches take what I have. My husband takes good care of me. Anything that I want is at my fingertips. All I have to do is pick up the phone and ask and in return I play the good wife. I don't sit around here and wait for him to come home. I have my own life and if he ever wanted to leave me for one of his tramps, it would have cost him. And trust me, he didn't want to part with any of his precious money."

Alverez was surprised by her demeanor. She was expecting Mrs. Lockett to be some weak, impressionable woman that didn't have a clue as to what her husband was really doing. Yvette was far from that. Alverez had spoken with Marcus and already knew of his lifestyle. Now Alverez was really curious as to what she was doing that her husband didn't know about. "You say that you had your own life, does that mean that you were seeing someone also" Alverez inquired? "No Detective. Unlike me, my husband wouldn't have been able to handle that."

Alverez was now becoming more and more intrigued by this conversation. "How do you know that for sure" Alverez asked. "Because my husband made it a point to put it in our prenuptial agreement. If I was ever found to be unfaithful, I wouldn't get a dime of his money in the event that he passed or divorced me. Detective, I don't know a man on God's green earth that is worth that price." I know that's right, Alverez thought to herself.

"Do you know what was in your husband's will," asked Alverez? "His brother Brandon gets sole ownership of the business and I get everything else. All the money and property we have," Yvette said with a slight smile. "Just out of curiosity, what does that consist of," she further inquired. "Roughly, two hundred million dollars, three houses, five cars and a yacht. She knew that right off the top of her head, maybe I'm not sorry for her loss, Alverez thought to herself. She amused herself with that thought, which caused her to smile slightly herself.

"Well, Mrs. Lockett, if you think of anything else that would assist me in finding your husband's killer please give me a call," as she handed her a business card (she noticed that Yvette used her left hand to receive the card). "Certainly Detective. I trust that you know your way out," said Yvette. "Certainly, Mrs. Lockett. Again, please accept my condolences." Detective Alverez started to walk out, then stopped and turned around "by the way, I love your shoes, what size are they," "Size nine" she replied. "Really...have a good day."

A.D. White

Chapter Eleven
Bringing Home Trouble

The next day all the detectives in the squad met to discuss the case. "Marcus, where are we with this investigation," asked the Lieutenant? "Well Lieu, I talked to the victim's brother, Brandon Lockett. Apparently, Nicholas had the business smarts and Brandon had the technical know-how. Brandon inherits Nicholas' share of the business which is motive enough." "Do we like him for the murder," the lieutenant inquired? "Yeah, he's still a suspect. It's more to him than meets the eye and money is always a strong motive. Also I caught him in a lie."

"What lie," asked the Lieutenant? "At the beginning of our conversation he tells me that he didn't know that his brother had the penthouse. As I was leaving, he asked me if I knew how the killer got the key and code to access the penthouse elevator." "Okay, I get it," said Sarge. "If he didn't know about the penthouse, how would he know that it took a key and code to access the elevator to the penthouse." "Exactly," replied Marcus. "The only thing that's bothering me is that they both have more money than they could possibly spend in a lifetime. Why kill your brother for more of what you already have?"

I also briefly talked to his personal assistant and mistress Nicole. Gotta do a little more digging there. Got the feeling that she's gonna be a wealth of information," said Marcus. "I want Callahan to interview her," instructed the Lieutenant.

The Lieutenant looked at Alverez "what did you get from the wife?" "The wife knew that her husband was banging his personal assistant but chose to turn a blind eye to it as long as it didn't affect her inheritance. They had a prenump that stipulated that if she was unfaithful, she wouldn't inherit any money but it didn't mention what would happen if he was unfaithful. She tried to sell me that she was content to maintain her lifestyle and didn't mind his playful ways," said Alverez. "I'm sensing that you didn't believe her," asked Marcus? "She gained all his money and property because of his death, so that seems motive enough to me."

"So is she a suspect," asked Sergeant U? "I can't rule her out sarge. She had everything to gain by his death. With him gone, it's all hers now. She can do whatever she wants. She doesn't need his permission. Now she can spend whatever she wants, see anyone she wants and can go anywhere she wants. She's a tall blonde beauty with her own money. She's a free woman now. Last, but not least, she had a coldness about her. The personal assistant that he was screwing used to be her best friend," Alverez responded. "Okay, follow her for a day or two. Let's see if she has anything to hide and then re-interview her," instructed the Lieutenant. Alverez nodded and said "copy Lieu."

"Tall and blonde," Marcus asked. "Yeah, not quite what I expected though" responded Alverez. "The personal assistant is tall and blonde also. I got a feeling that we know what his type is now. The receptionist is also tall and blonde, goes by the name Ashley. She was kinda flirty. I think that Logan should interview her," said Marcus. "He has a way of extracting information out of beautiful women," Marcus laughed. Logan playfully threw his hands up in the air "Hey, don't hate the playa..."

The lieutenant looked at Callahan, "did you interview the management at the building?" Detective Callahan stood up, "yes sir. There are a total of four concierges that work twelve hour shifts each. Stanley Richards began his shift at 2300 hours Saturday night until 1100 hours Sunday morning. One can conclude that he was on duty at the time of this repugnant offense. Absent the killer surreptitiously entering the building, Stanley should be aware of information detrimental to our case."

Logan interrupted "so Professor, are you saying that Stanley was there that night and must know something because the killer had to go past his desk?" "That's exactly what I'm alluding to Logan." "Damn, why couldn't you have just said it then," Logan asked in playful disgust as the squad members erupted in laughter.

"Which brings me to the fact that the lobby has a camera. I looked at the tape and at 0100 hours, while Stanley the concierge was conveniently away from his desk, someone enters the lobby and walks in the direction of the penthouse elevator. Interestingly enough, the person is wearing an oversized jacket with a hat and looks like they're trying to conceal their identity," said Detective Callahan. Lieutenant O'Malley asks "could that person be a woman?" "Could be sir. I took a copy of the tape to forensics to see if they can clean it up and give us a few still pictures of our mystery person." "Good job Callahan," said the lieutenant. Callahan smiled as he sat back down and looked over at Logan and nodded.

"Alright, bring Stanley the concierge in for an interview. I want Marcus and Logan to go at him." Marcus and Logan both nodded in agreement. "Anything else," asked the Lieutenant? "We have a business rival named Diedrick Becker who unsuccessfully tried to take the victim's business. The brother thinks that this Becker dude is capable of murder so we'll have him in for an interview also." "Sounds like there's no shortage of suspects in this case," joked Logan. "Lastly, the victim had a driver. He's not a suspect yet, but he should be able to help us trace the victim's whereabouts prior to his murder." "Keep me posted," said the Lieutenant as he walked out of the squad room.

"Hey Sarge, what's going on with Big Russ," Logan asked? "We sure could use his help on this. We got more suspects than we can shake a stick at." "L.T. made him take a non-optional vacation. He should be back Monday morning. I called him a couple of times but he didn't answer. Time to call it a day ladies and germs, see you in the a.m."

The squad members went to their desks and prepared to leave for the day. Logan asked Marcus, "what's for dinner tonight?" "What, you inviting yourself over for a meal," asked Marcus. "Yup," Logan responded, "I'm the only friend that you've got that Gina likes. Plus, I haven't seen the boys in a minute. They could benefit from my calming demeanor and steady influence."

Marcus laughed, "man, you're full of it. Your fridge is empty, isn't it?" "Yup," he responded, "a brother's got to eat." "What, none of your ladies know how to cook," asked Marcus. "All my ladies cook, that's a pre-requisite," said Logan. "Okay, I gotta make a run before I head home. Meet me at the house at seven. I'll call Gina and let her know that I'm bringing home trouble," Marcus joked. "Everything alright? You seem a little distracted lately," Logan asked? "I'm fine, just got an errand to run, see you at seven," said Marcus.

When Marcus arrived at home he was dog tired. He opened the front door and was greeted by his two boys, MJ (Marcus Junior) and Brandon, who were nine and ten years old. They both ran up to him and hugged him tight around his legs. "How's my men doing" Marcus asked. Brandon responded, "MJ took my video game." "No I didn't," responded MJ. Gina walked out of the kitchen to the front door "boys, give your dad a minute. Let him come in and relax before you start telling on each other. Time for homework until dinner is ready," as she pointed down the hall. "Okay," they pouted and ran down the hall as Gina yelled "walk not run."

Gina walked up to Marcus and gently touched his waist as she gave him a peck on the lips. "How's my man doing," she asked? "I'm good Boo, but it's been a long day. You don't mind the extra mouth for dinner," he asked. "Well, now that you mention it," as Gina smiled and started to laugh. Marcus just looked at her and smiled. "The boy needs a home cooked meal, you know those women of his can't cook." "I know babe, Logan's always welcome here. Tell him he can't bring anymore of his skanks here though."

Marcus bent down and took off his shoes "what's on the menu," he asked? "Fried fish, mash potatoes and greens" she responded. "Umh, that's my favorite," said Marcus. "Everything's your favorite" Gina responded as she walked back to the kitchen to finish cooking. Marcus looked at her as she walked away and said, "now that's my favorite" as he pointed to her rear end. Gina looked back and said "you so nasty Marcus" then mumbled "but

I love it." Marcus said "I heard that," and laughed. "Meet me in the bedroom around 10 p.m." Marcus continued. "Promises, promises," responded Gina in a playful manner.

Marcus went to the bedroom, took off his clothes and showered. Once changed, he heard the doorbell. Marcus looked through the peephole, then opened the door. "What's up bro," said Logan and gave him a man hug. "Come on in," Marcus responded as MJ and Brandon ran to the door, yelling "Uncle Logan" and jumped on him. Logan fell to the ground as if the boys were strong enough to tackle him. "Man you boys pack a punch," said Logan as all three rolled around on the floor. "Okay boys, let Logan up. If you break him, I'll have to pay his medical bills," joked Marcus. Logan got up and the boys ran off.

Gina came to the door with a spatula in her hand. Logan opened his arms wide and said "honey, I'm home." Gina laughed and shook her head as she gave him a hug. "You're a mess Logan. I hope you're hungry" she commented. "I'm always hungry Sis," Logan said as he started walking down the hall. Gina turned around and looked down at Logan's shoes in disgust. Logan stopped dead in his tracks, "I know. I'm taking them off," as he bent down and took off his shoes and mumbled "a little dirt never killed nobody."

"Why you mumbling Detective, speak up," said Gina. "I was just saying your food never killed nobody Gina," responded Logan. "Okay Logan, keep playing. See if you get invited back for another meal," said Gina. Logan mumbled something else, but Gina didn't pay him any mind this time.

Marcus and Logan walked down the hall to his office while Gina finished preparing their meal. "What's your thoughts on the case," asked Logan? "Some would have me think that this murder was strictly business, but I not buying that. This was emotional. My gut tells me that he was killed out of jealousy or love. Two of the strongest motives there are," said Marcus. "Yeah, I'm thinking the same way," said Logan. "So that points us in the direction of the wife and the mistress/personal assistant," Logan continued. "They're definitely the front runners, but let's see if there's more after you talk to the receptionist Ashley. I got a feeling that she knows everything that goes on at that place," said Marcus. "She's also tall and blonde which we now know is his type. I wouldn't be surprised if he was hitting that too."

"Damn, ole boy had it like that," Logan asked with a surprised tone? Marcus continued, "this guy had good looks and plenty of money which makes men feel invincible. And it's an aphrodisiac to a lot of women. After working this job for all these years Logan," Marcus shook his head "very little surprises me. Money is the root of all evil and Nicholas Lockett had plenty of both."

Chapter Twelve
Monday Morning

Monday morning roll call came and went and Detective Anthony Russo was nowhere to be found. The lieutenant made him take a week of leave to get himself together. To seek help or put in his retirement papers. Big Russ was a liability and starting to be an embarrassment. Being drunk on duty wouldn't shed a good light on the police department or instill confidence from the public's perspective. After several calls of his went unanswered, Sergeant U sent Marcus and Logan to go to Big Russ' home to check on his welfare.

When they pulled up to Big Russ' home, they saw his car in the driveway and everything appeared to be normal. They slowly walked to the front door and knocked. After repeated knocks and no answer, they were scared of what was to come next. Even though they didn't discuss it on the ride over, in the back of their minds they wondered if Big Russ had harmed himself. He wouldn't be the first cop to eat his gun. Logan stepped down off the porch and slowly walked over to the living room window to look inside. He slowly placed his face against the window pane and peered inside. What he saw startled him so that he lost his balance and fell backwards onto the ground, which in turn startled Marcus.

Then the front door opened and Big Russ emerged. "What are you, a fucking peeping Tom" Russ jokingly yelled. When Logan looked into the window he saw Big Russ on the other side looking back at him which surprised him and sent him reeling backwards. "You're a sight for sore eyes big boy" blurted out Marcus while giving him a big hug.

"Logan, get off your ass and come on" said Russ. Logan was happy to see Big Russ alive and well but irritated that he fell and soiled the seat of his pants. He got up and gave Russ a hug also "damn, see what you did. You owe me for the cleaning bill" said Logan as he began to wipe the dirt off his rear. Russ slapped Logan on the ass and said "a little dirty ass ain't never hurt nobody. What are you guys doing here?"

"You didn't show up for roll call so Sarge asked us to check on you" said Marcus. "Well I figured it was no reason to go to roll call gentlemen. I think that I've worked my last shift on the Police Department" said Russ. "Really! You're ready to give all this up" Logan said sarcastically. "Yeah, it's time. I've been running from this for a few years now. I guess I was scared and still am. Even though I know it's time, it's hard to give up something that you've been doing for over thirty years. This is all I've known. The big question is, what's next" said Russ. Marcus and Logan searched for an answer, but looked dumbfounded.

Big Russ continued "that's what I've been thinking about this past week. Making a plan for the second part of my life." "What did you come up with" asked Logan? Big Russ smiled "first and foremost, I went to AA. Believe it or not guys, I've may have a drinking problem." "Nah, not you" Marcus and Logan jokingly said in unison. Big Russ laughed and said "you guys can bite my big white ass. No bullshit guys, it's been hard since my wife left. We didn't have any children and loneliness can be a man's worst friend. I gotta get a handle on this drinking thing."

"Been sober now for five days and counting." "Good Russ, man I'm happy for you" said Marcus. Russ continued "this may surprise you, but I've got an appointment with a therapist." Logan jumped in "finally gonna deal with that masturbation problem you've got?" Logan could hardly get that sentence out because he was laughing so hard. "Oh, you just crack yourself up, don't you" said Marcus. "A lot of times, we cops don't reach out for help. We feel like we're big and bad and can do it all by ourselves. There's no shame in asking for help" said Russ.

"You're right man, we can all learn from you" said Marcus. "Come over to the house this Sunday and watch the Skins-Cowboys game with us" pointing to Logan. Logan interrupted "Marcus, I still don't know how you're from D.C. and can be a Cowboys fan" he said with contempt. "I don't know how you can root for such a sorry team" Marcus fired back. "Okay ladies" Russ interrupted "this conversation was about me" he said jokingly. "I'll meet you guys at the station. Gotta talk to the lieutenant, then go to H.R. and put my papers in. Today is the first day of the rest of my life."

Chapter Thirteen
Diedrick Becker

Mr. Diedrick Becker was contacted and asked to come in for an interview. He was represented by a tall, slim, sexy Latina attorney named Sandra Leon. Educated at Georgetown Law School and had a propensity to represent less than law abiding citizens. Marcus and Logan conducted the interview while the sergeant and lieutenant observed from the deck.

Mr. Becker was thirty-five years old, a little over six feet tall with a slim build. Well dressed in what looked like a tailored suit with his black hair combed to the rear. Thin black mustache with lightly acne scarred cheeks. If there was such a thing as the German Mafia, he'd fit the bill.

Marcus: Good morning Mr. Becker and Attorney Leon. My name is Detective Marcus Rose and this is Detective Logan Steele. We are investigating the murder of Mr. Nicholas Lockett.

Attorney Leon: Good Morning Detectives. Is my client a suspect or a witness?

Marcus: He's not a suspect at this time counselor. We are hoping that your client can help us develop suspects or witnesses.

Attorney Leon: That's noted Detective. Just be aware that we reserve the right to end this interview at any time.

Attorney Leon removed a document from her brief case and placed it on the table.

Attorney Leon: You should also know that my client is listed as a consul of the German Government and as such is afforded Diplomatic Immunity. Not that we think it will be necessary in this case.

Marcus and Logan looked at each other in amazement and disgust. The interview was barely underway and they felt like that had just been bitch slapped.

Marcus looked over the document for a few minutes.

Marcus: Mr. Becker, how did you know Nicholas Lockett?

Mr. Becker: He was a business rival of mine.

Marcus: Our information shows that you tried to take over Mr. Lockett's business. Were you successful?

Mr. Becker: Detective, I'm sure that you already know the answer to that question, but I'll play your little game. It didn't go well. Somehow he found out about my intentions and blocked my efforts.

Marcus: Did that cause tension between the two of you?

Mr. Becker: Somewhat.

Logan: Let's stop beating around the bush and get straight to the point Mr. Becker. I'm told that you hated Nicholas Lockett.

Mr. Becker: That would be putting it lightly (he said with a cold look in his eyes)

Logan: Why such an intense hate over business? Or was it more than just business?

Mr. Becker: Once again, I'm sure that you know the answer to that also. Business is one thing, but defiling a man's wife is another. He corrupted my Angel!

Logan: Now we're getting to the good stuff!

Marcus: By Angel, do you mean your wife?

Mr. Becker: Yes.

Marcus: How did you find out about the affair?

Mr. Becker: I had my suspicions, so I had her followed. They went right to his little penthouse playpen.

Marcus: The same penthouse that he was killed at?

Attorney Leon: I don't like where this is going. I'm going to have to stop this line of questioning Detectives. This interview is over.

Marcus: Why counselor? Your client has diplomatic immunity. There's no way possible that the truth can hurt him.

Mr. Becker: He's right. Let's continue because this is the first and last time that I will answer any of these questions. Make it good Detective. You're only getting one shot at this.

Attorney Leon: I advise you against this (as she looked at her client). Continuing with this line of questioning is not in your best interest.

Mr. Becker: I hear you, but I'm a big boy. Let's continue (as he looked at Marcus).

Marcus: What is your wife's name Mr. Becker?

Mr. Becker: Angelika Becker.

Marcus: Angelika. That means Angel in German and your name (Diedrick) means Gifted Ruler. So when Nicholas Lockett screwed the Gifted Ruler's angel, did that make you want to kill him?

Mr. Becker: You damn right it did.

Attorney Leon: Mr. Becker, I must insist that you stop talking immediately.

Mr. Becker: You work for me. I hear your objection, now you be quiet!

Attorney Leon: Apparently you don't want or need my counsel and I refuse to sit here and watch you incriminate yourself against my advice. (She got up and left the room at that time).

Logan: Now that you're handler is gone, let's continue.

Mr. Becker: Let's.

Marcus: I asked you before I was so rudely interrupted, did the fact that Nicholas Lockett did nasty, filthy things to your little Angel make you wanna kill him?

Mr. Becker: Yes, It made me wanna kill him. I hated his fucking guts. I would have liked nothing more than to put a bullet in his head and watch him die but someone beat me to it. I applaud whoever killed him. They should build a statue of that person.

Logan: Tell us how you really feel (he said sarcastically).

Marcus: So are you saying that you didn't kill him or have him killed?

Mr. Becker: No, I didn't. That's why I don't need my diplomatic immunity. As you well know, wanting to kill someone is not a crime!

Logan: Why should we believe you?

Mr. Becker: Because I'm telling the truth. And actually, I don't give a shit if you believe me or not. Fuck you and Nicholas Lockett!

Logan: I love it when you talk dirty (he said with a smile).

Marcus: Where's your wife at now?

Mr. Becker: She's in Frankfurt. I sent her back to Germany. There's no way I could allow her to stay here after embarrassing me like that.

Marcus: Just a guess, but is your wife tall and blonde?

Mr. Becker: Yeah, how'd you know?

The Root Of All Evil

Marcus: Just a guess.

Mr. Becker: I'm done talking now. Can I leave?

Marcus: You're free to go Mr. Becker.

Logan: Don't leave town though. We may want to talk to you again. (Logan looked at Marcus) I always wanted to say that.

Mr. Becker: Yeah right, auf wiedersehen (he said with a smirk on his face).

Mr. Becker was shown the way out of the building. Lieutenant O'Malley and Sergeant U approached Marcus and Logan. "Good interview gentlemen, but do we believe him" asked the Lieutenant? "I think he did it" replied Logan. "Me too" said Sergeant U. They all looked at Marcus.

"I don't know. He has the means and a motive. He knew where the penthouse was. He has diplomatic immunity. Why not just admit it, if he did it?" "By the way" said the Lieutenant, "I had Callahan check with the Secret Service. They were telling the truth about his immunity." "How'd you find out about the wife" asked Sergeant U? "An old C.I. of mine named Freddie got me that information. Not sure how he got it, but it turned out to be true" said Logan. Logan looked at Marcus "how'd you know all that shit about Diedrick meaning

Gifted Ruler and Angelika meaning Angel." Marcus grinned "man you'd be surprised of all the useless information I've got in this head. Every once in a while it comes in handy."

Chapter Fourteen
Have You Ever Seen a Wise Young Man

Marcus and Logan wanted to talk to Nicolas Lockett's driver. They knew he would be a wealth of information. Being the driver of a very wealthy man had its perks. First of all, you'll be paid handsomely to keep his secrets. Discretion is a virtue but it's not cheap. The driver would know where he was every minute of every day. Most of all he'd know where all the bodies were buried. Not literally, just meaning that he would know all the things that Nicholas Lockett didn't want anyone else to know. Things the driver could see and overhear could be damaging if found out by the wrong people and having a loyal driver is imperative.

Marcus had the phone number of the driver but for some reason he never answered his cell phone. He got the feeling that the driver was trying to avoid speaking to him which only made Marcus more determined to have that conversation. The driver's name was Stephan Richardson and he chauffeured Mr. Lockett around in a black 2016 Cadillac Escalade. The Escalade was Stephan's office per se. They couldn't find him at his home or the business address so they followed their hunch and looked for him at the Lockett residence.

Sure enough Stephan was sitting behind the wheel in front of the Lockett's garage area. Marcus walked up to the driver's side and knocked on the window. Stephan rolled down the window and asked "can I help you?" Marcus raised his identification up to Stephan's eye level and said "I'm Detective Marcus Steele from the D.C. Police's Homicide Division and I'd like to talk to you." "I don't wanna talk to you" was his response as he started the vehicle and put his hand on the gear lever to put it in drive.

Logan walked in front of the vehicle to prevent Stephan from driving away. Still in park, Stephan revved up the engine to persuade him to move. Marcus removed his 9mm Glock from his holster and pointed it at Stephan's head "if you hit my partner with that four thousand pound weapon you're driving, I'm gonna shoot you in that big head of yours. Now turn the car off and step out of the vehicle." Stephan turned the car off but sat there in silence. Marcus holstered his weapon, opened the driver's side door, grabbed him by his shirt and attempted to pull him out but he didn't budge. Logan walked over and assisted him. It took the strength of both men to pull Stephan out of the car.

Both men looked up to him as he stood there. Six feet six inches in height, weighing in at two hundred and ninety pounds. Marcus and Logan were no small men, but this guy was massive. It was obvious that when he wasn't driving, he was in the gym lifting weights. Marcus had been on the Police Department a long time and the older that you get, the more you use your brain and not your muscles to get someone to comply. So he tried to appeal to Stephan's intellectual side (if he had one). "Listen, all we want to do is talk to you. It's not gonna take long and we'll have you back here in no time" said Marcus. "I don't wanna go to the police station, why can't you talk to me right here" Stephan asked. Marcus replied "that's not the way we do things. It would be in all our best interest if you were to cooperate."

Now Logan wasn't at that stage yet. He was still young and healthy and still relied on physicality and intimidation to get the job done. "Listen big boy. We can do this the easy way or the hard way and it makes no difference to me which one you choose" said Logan. Marcus thought to himself (damn Logan, why'd you have to say that).

Just then, Stephan forcibly pushed Logan in his chest area with both arms, forcing him back and causing him to lose his balance. Stephan then swung his left arm around, attempting to strike Marcus in the face with his elbow. As Marcus ducked, Stephan's elbow struck the rear driver's side window of the Escalade, causing it to shatter. Marcus then drove his right foot into the back of Stephan's left knee, forcing him to the ground on both his knees. Logan had re-gained his balance by then and struck Stephan in the face with a left uppercut and a right hook which didn't seem to faze him at all.

Marcus and Logan both had that "Oh Shit" look on their faces as Stephan rose to his feet. Logan attempted to hit him with a straight right, which Stephan caught with his left hand. Marcus then jumped on his back, reaching around to place him in a choke hold. They both fell to the concrete as Marcus held on for dear life. Stephan's arms and legs were flailing as he attempted to break free. Logan grabbed one of his arms in an attempt to place hand cuffs on him. All three struggled for a minute or two before Yvette Lockett ran outside screaming for Stephan to stop and let them hand cuff him. Stephan immediately stopped and complied with her wishes.

Ten minutes later, Stephan was now handcuffed and sitting in the back of a police wagon. Marcus still out of breath and leaning against their unmarked cruiser. You could hear Marcus mumble "I'm too old for this crap." Marcus told the transport officer that Stephan was under arrest for assault on a police officer and to take him to the Homicide Division for processing. They would be there shortly.

As the wagon drove away, Marcus looked at Logan and asked "was that necessary?" "What do you mean" responded Logan. "I'm talking to the guy to convince him to comply and you piss him off by trying to bully him. A couple of minutes more and I could have talked him right into a pair of handcuffs without a single punch being thrown. But you jump the gun and now we gotta fight the Jolly White Giant. And we'd be still fighting him right now if Mrs. Lockett didn't run out and calm his butt down" said Marcus.

Logan didn't really get what Marcus was trying to convey to him and responded with "I could see that talking nice to him really wasn't going to work so I wanted to be a little more forceful." "Let me explain something to you" said Marcus. "Have you ever wondered why God gives strength to the young guys and wisdom to the older ones? When you're younger, you can do all that fighting crap. You can chase people around and depend on your strength and speed.

As you get older, you learn to police smarter. You can catch more bees with honey than with vinegar." "Okay Marcus, next time we'll do it your way. When your sweet talk doesn't work, then I'll hit em." Marcus just shook his head and said "answer me this genius. Have you ever seen a wise young man?" Logan had no response. "I didn't think so" responded Marcus. "The beginning of wisdom is realizing how little you really know."

Chapter Fifteen
Stanley the Concierge

A week had passed with minimal progress on the case. It was time to shake the tree and see who else fell out. Marcus loved doing interviews and interrogations. It was like mental aerobics. Out smarting the suspect and tripping him or her up with their own words. It was now time to talk to Stanley the concierge. Marcus couldn't shake the feeling that he had something to do with this. Yeah, he had been cooperative, but that didn't mean that his hands were totally clean and today was the day to find out. He wasn't a suspect yet, so they didn't have to read him his rights or ask him if he wanted a lawyer. Marcus and Logan locked their guns away and walked Stanley to the interview room.

Stanley was an older guy, about fifty five years old. Hair receding in the front and a touch of gray on the sides. 5'9" with a medium build. He wore a pair of tan Khaki's with a white pull over shirt with buttons. Looked real conservative. As the door closed, Marcus flipped the switch on the wall that started videotaping the interview.

Marcus: Have a seat Stanley (as he pointed to the chair on the other side of the table). We've met before, but I'd like to re-introduce myself. My name is Detective

Marcus Rose and this is my partner, Detective Logan Steele. (Stanley reached out and shook Marcus' hand, then Logan's).

Stanley: I...I remember, anything I can do to help you guys, just ask.

Marcus sat down, reached into his inside jacket pocket, removed his hand sanitizer and cleaned his hands. Stanley reached into his pants pocket and removed an inhaler. Placed it to his mouth and squirted a burst.

Marcus: Asthma?

Stanley: Yeah, it only acts up when I'm nervous.

Marcus: No need to be nervous Stanley but there are a couple of details about this murder that are bothering me.

Stanley was obviously nervous and just looked at Marcus, waiting for his question.

Marcus: First, state your full name.

Stanley: Uh...Stanley, Stanley Richardson.

Marcus: Stanley, we're just looking for all the facts so we can put together a time line. I want to know what time you came to work and everything that you did that night, until you left in the morning.

Stanley: Well, I really didn't do much. I got to work at eleven o'clock Saturday night and I sat at my desk until I brought Mr. Lockett his paper, around 10:30 am Sunday morning.

Logan: So Stanley, you would have us believe that you sat at your desk for eleven and a half hours, without getting up and leaving your desk at all? Hell, a man your age probably has to go pee every few hours.

Stanley: Well yeah, I got up a few times to go to the bathroom. The door to the bathroom is directly behind my desk. I couldn't have been gone for more than two minutes each time.

Marcus: What time did Mr. Lockett go to the penthouse and was anyone with him?

Stanley: About twelve thirty that night and he was alone.

Logan: How many ways are there to get to the penthouse?

Stanley: Two ways. There's the penthouse elevator and the penthouse stairwell.

Logan: Exactly, and to get to both, someone has to walk by your desk?

Stanley: Yes

Marcus: Did anyone go to his penthouse either before he arrived or after?

Stanley: Well, I don't know if anyone went to the penthouse before I started at eleven, but no one else went to the penthouse when I was there except Mr. Lockett.

Logan: Just by the simple fact that Mr. Lockett was murdered in his apartment, means that someone else had to be there. He didn't murder himself Stanley.

Stanley: Well...I see what you're saying, but no one came past my desk and went to the penthouse elevator or stairwell. Other guests and residents came in at different times, but no one used the penthouse access.

Marcus: Someone entered Mr. Lockett's penthouse that night and the only way to get to the penthouse elevator is to walk past your desk, summon the elevator with a key, then enter a code to be taken upstairs. You need the same key and code access to enter the penthouse stairwell also.

Stanley was silent. He wasn't sure if that was a question or not.

Marcus: Would it surprise you to know that we looked at the footage of the tape that night and at one in the morning, someone walked past your desk. The camera pans from left to right and when the camera came back around to the penthouse elevator and stairs, the person was gone. Which means that they had to use either one.

Stanley: Am I gonna need a lawyer gentlemen?

Logan: That's up to you Stanley, but before you decide that, you gotta understand that once you request a lawyer, we can't question you anymore tonight. We can't get your story or your help in solving this case and all we're trying to do is solve a murder.

Stanley: I'm starting to get the feeling that you think that I had something to do with this.

Marcus: Did you?

Stanley: Of course not. I would never hurt Mr. Lockett or anyone else.

Marcus: Well good Stanley. Now that we got that out of the way...cause you know that I had to ask you that...do you know of anyone that wanted to harm him?

Stanley: No, absolutely not.

Marcus: Let's get back to the mystery person that walked past your desk at one a.m. Strangely enough, you weren't at your desk at that time. Must have been one of your bathroom breaks, huh?

Stanley: Coincidently, it must have been.

Marcus: Stanley, very few things in this life are truly coincidence.

Logan: Coincidence my ass (as Logan slammed his fist down on the table). Is it also a coincidence that the same person left thirty minutes later and you weren't at your desk that time either?

Stanley: Oh, what is this? Bad cop, bad cop?

Logan: That's real clever Stanley. Let me tell you what's gonna happen when I find out that you conveniently left your desk so that someone could go upstairs and murder Mr. Lockett. Cause that's what I think you did. We're gonna lock your ass up for being an accessory before the fact, which makes you just as guilty as the person that killed him. Then we're gonna send your ass to the pokey. Do you know why they call it the pokey?

Stanley: No (as he crossed his arms).

Logan: Because once you're in jail, someone's gonna make you their bitch. They're going to pass you around and poke you all night long. You're gonna be Bubba's bitch.

Marcus: Stanley, tell us what really happened. The person that walked by your desk while you were AWOL was wearing an oversized jacket and hat and they did a pretty good job of concealing their identity. Where did they get the key to summons the elevator and the code to ride it to the penthouse? Oh and did I forget to mention that same person exited the lobby fifteen minutes later. That's our dilemma Stanley. We're going to find out who it was eventually and they're gonna try to make a deal by telling us about everyone that helped them. So I suggest that you make a deal first. Because once they sell you out, we're not going to need you then. Which means it'll be too late for any deals and off to the pokey you go!

Logan: Oh, and lest me no forget to mention that Mr. Lockett was a very influential man and the U.S. Attorneys will probably seek the death penalty on this one. You can't go around killing rich people Stanley!

Stanley: I'd like to seek legal counsel at this time.

Marcus: Okay Stanley, I got what I need from you for now. You're free to leave and we'll be in touch with your counsel right before we lock your butt up.

Stanley looked shaken as he rose from his chair and left the room. He was confused and started walking in the wrong direction to leave. "Stanley...that way" as Marcus pointed in the direction he needed to go to leave the building. Logan grinned "that death penalty remarked really got him shook." "Yeah, too bad he doesn't know that D.C. doesn't have the death penalty."

Chapter Sixteen
Ashley

Marcus set up the date and time for Lockett Electronics receptionist Ashley, to come in and answer a few questions. One of the officers walked her to the detective's offices and introduced her to Logan. "Hi, I'm Ashley Lake and I'm here to see Detective Rose." Logan responded "Detective Rose is working on other matters and he asked me to talk to you. I'm Detective Logan Steele" as he extended his hand.

Ashley came in expecting Marcus, but was pleasantly surprised to speak with Logan. She smiled and peered into his eyes as she shook his hand. Ashley was 5'9" in height and loved tall men that she had to look up to and at 6'5", Logan was her cup of tea. Tall and handsome with a muscular body. She was wearing a tight fitting navy blue skirt with a pink blouse tucked neatly in at her waist.

As they shook, Logan cupped her hand with his other hand also and asked "Ms. Lake, do you mind if I call you Ashley?" Ashley couldn't help but notice how his large hands engulfed hers. "You may" she responded in a playful manner. "Let's go to the interview room where we can talk in private" said Logan as he pointed in the direction of the room. Ashley walked in front of

Logan giving him a perfect view of her assets. Once they entered the room, Logan pulled out her chair as she sat, exposing her well-shaped thighs. Instead of sitting across the table from her, Logan sat beside her on the same side of the table but left the door open.

There was a piece of paper on the table and Logan wrote the number 9 on it. Puzzled by that, Ashley asked "what's the nine mean." "That's my lucky number" he replied. "Oh, are you into numerology" she asked. "You could say so" he replied.

"Have you ever modeled" Logan asked. Ashley blushed "no, but I'm told that I have the look for it." "You do, but I won't let that distract me. I love your shoes, what size are they" Logan said in a flirtatious manner. She was taken aback by that question, but answered anyway "your lucky number."

"Now that we have that out of the way, let's get down to business. Often times in cases we try to learn everything we can about the victim and sometimes that information can help us in solving a case. My partner felt like you were someone that was very knowledgeable of the comings and goings of Lockett Electronics and might be able to assist us with developing a clear picture of the workplace." "Well, I do keep up with current events and I am willing to help you, Detective Steele" she replied. "I knew the minute I saw you, that you were valuable" Logan said with his signature devilish grin.

"What kind of person was Mr. Lockett? I'm told that he had an eye for the ladies. Was he seeing anyone at the office" Logan asked? "That would be his personal assistant Nicole" she responded, "the two of them were an item." "What was their relationship like" Logan asked? "She stuck to him like glue. Everywhere he went, there she was. She followed him around like a little puppy" responded Ashley. If he stopped too quickly, she'd probably run into the back of him" she joked. "Did you ever see them fight or have a disagreement" asked Logan? "No, quite frankly, he was an asshole, but she didn't seem to mind." "Really" Logan responded.

Ashley continued "he was very charming until you got to know him, then his true personality emerged." "Wow, tell me more" said Logan. "He was smart, good looking and rich but he had a dark soul." "What do you mean" asked Logan? "His wealth blinded women. It temporarily masked his true character unless you were much more interested in his money than his personality." "I kinda understand what you mean, but can you give me an example" asked Logan.

"Sure. He asked me to dinner about six months ago. I turned him down a couple of times but he wouldn't take no for an answer. He had a sense of entitlement. I finally agreed to go out without him just so he would stop asking. His assistant Nicole kept his schedule and all his appointments. Even though he was seeing her, he had her make the reservations for dinner with me. Then she starting giving me the evil eye and acting funky towards me, instead of being pissed at him." "Yeah, I don't get it either. A lot of times, women direct their anger at the wrong person."

"During dinner he talked a lot about his possessions. His cars, houses and all his grown man toys. I, I, I, everything was about him. I told him that I liked a man that was spiritual. Not a bible thumper, just a man that realized that his blessings came from God. You know, a humble man. I said to him that no one can serve two masters. You can't serve God and money. Can you guess how that Devil responded to that? He said then God is a luxury I can't afford."

After dinner I asked him to take me home. I was turned off by him and didn't want to continue the date. He had a driver and we were in the back seat. He started to get a little touchy feely and I pushed his hand away. It was obvious that he wasn't used to hearing no. His whole attitude changed. He got angry and tried to man handle me. He got on top of me and pinned me down. His asshole driver continued driving as if he couldn't see or hear what was going on in the back. He put his hand up my dress and started pulling down my panties. That's when I punched him in his damn throat. He fell back and was gasping for air.

Now all of a sudden, his driver slams on the brakes and I hop out of the truck just as fast as I can. Before I slam the door shut, I tell him that if he ever touched me again, I would kill his privileged ass." "Wow, what happened the next time that you saw him at work" Logan asked. "Nothing. He acted as if nothing ever happened between us and he knew that if he tried to fire me I would own his company" she replied. "Did you report it to the police or tell anybody about it" asked Logan. "No" she replied. "I believe in karma. I'm sure that I wasn't the only person that he ever tried that with. I knew that sooner or later the day would come when someone would slash his throat. I can't say that it surprised me."

"He wasn't my type anyway" she said with a smile. "What is your type" asked Logan? "You know how a man treats a woman when he wants to take her to bed" asked Ashley? Logan nodded yes. "I like a man that treats you the same way after he gets what he wants. I'm not into men that chase women for sport." Ashley looked Logan up and down and said "and I like em tall...with big hands" as she flashed a devilish grin.

Logan smiled back "one last questions. Who do you think killed Mr. Lockett?" "I don't know Detective but I'll bet you anything that it was a woman. Or maybe a jealous husband or boyfriend." "Well, thank you Ashley, you have been very helpful" as he stood. Ashley remained seated as she reached into her purse and removed a pen and her business card. She turned it over to the back and wrote down her phone number and handed Logan the card as she stood. "Here's my personal cell phone number. Feel free to call me if I can be of further assistance to you Detective." Logan accepted the card and put it in his pants pocket "I think that further questioning might be in order. Thanks again, and oh...have you ever been to Mr. Lockett's penthouse?" "No, never" she replied.

Chapter Seventeen
Nicole

It was time to talk to Nicholas Lockett's mistress Nicole. Marcus conferred with the lieutenant and they decided that Detective Callahan should interview her. She seemed to be of discerning taste and they figured that she would relate to Callahan better than anyone else in the squad. Callahan greeted her at the entrance to the Detective's office "Hi, my name is Detective Frank Callahan, you must be Nicole" as he extended his hand. "Yes, Nicole Carrington, nice to meet you Detective" as she shook his hand. "Likewise" responded Callahan as he walked her to the interview room. Marcus, Logan and the lieutenant were watching from the observation deck.

Callahan closed the door and flipped the switch on the wall that started videotaping the interview. "I am obligated to inform you that this interview is being recorded Ms. Carrington." Nicole nodded in agreement. "I just met you but it's obvious to me that you are still in mourning. Are you Okay" asked Callahan? "I'm okay" responded Nicole. "Can I get you anything to drink? Water, soda?" Nicole shook her head no. Callahan continued "first let me say that I'm very sorry for your loss." "The world lost a great man" responded Nicole.

Callahan was a little taken back by her overstatement, but kept his composure.

Callahan: Can you tell me about Nicholas? What kind of man was he?

Nicole: He was a hard worker and a dedicated family man.

Callahan: Did he have any children?

Nicole: No, just a wife...and his brother.

Callahan: So by dedicated, you mean that he was dedicated to his wife?

Nicole: Yes, and his company.

Callahan: Well Nicole, I hate to contradict your assessment of Mr. Lockett, but all the information that I've received leads me to believe that he was an avaricious person.

Nicole: Only people who didn't know him well shared that opinion. Yes, he loved his money, but what rich man doesn't?

Callahan: Show me a rich man and I'll show you a hypocrite!

Nicole: Show me a poor man and I'll show you an underachiever!

Callahan: (he smiled) Touché. Who do you think committed this crime?

Nicole: (without hesitation) His wife.

Callahan: You said he was a dedicated family man, what reason would his wife have to kill him?

Nicole: She paused and seemed to be choosing her words carefully. They lived two separate lives. She didn't like the fact that Nicholas worked all the time and they rarely saw each other. Not to mention the fact that she was jealous of our relationship.

Callahan: Did she have a reason to be jealous of you?

Nicole: Let me be truthful with you Detective...

Callahan: That would be nice.

Nicole: I wasn't just his personal assistant. I was also his lover. She couldn't give him what he needed so I did her job also. I see the way that you're looking at me. Don't judge me Detective. You have no idea how hard I've worked.

Callahan: I'm not judging you Nicole. I understand. In fact, it sounds like you were doing her a favor. You took care of the things that she couldn't or wouldn't do for him.

Nicole: Exactly!

Callahan: I know that he trusted and depended on you to run his affairs.

Nicole: Yes, without me, he didn't know where he was supposed to be on any given day. He had a busy schedule and I made sure he was where he was supposed to be and at the time he was supposed to be there.

Callahan: Sounds like a burdensome responsibility.

Nicole: I kept busy, but it was no burden. I enjoyed making his life easier.

Callahan: And what did you get in return for your hard work?

Nicole: His admiration and love, not to mention a substantial paycheck.

Callahan: Love?

Nicole: Yes, we were in love.

Callahan: Did he ever tell you that he loved you?

Nicole: No. He didn't have to but I could tell by the way that he treated me.

Callahan: Okay (as he thought to himself "Obviously delusional"). Did he ever buy you clothes or shoes?

Nicole: Yes, both.

Callahan: What size shoe do you wear?

Nicole: You never ask a woman's age or shoe size detective, but if you must know, I wear a size 9.

 Did his wife know the extent of your relationship?

Nicole: Yes. At one point she became suspicious of our relationship and asked me directly if we were sleeping together. Since we used to be friends, I felt like I owed her the truth.

Callahan: Really? How did she take the news?

Nicole: She wasn't happy. What wife would be? She just wanted to know if we had made love in their house. I assured her that we had not. I told her that we had a penthouse for that. You know, just to ease her mind.

Callahan: Your kindness abounds.

Nicole flashed a smug grin.

Callahan: Did you have the key and code to the elevator?

Nicole: I saw him put the code in before, but I didn't have a key. He wouldn't give anyone a spare key to Bat Cave.

Callahan: Bat Cave?

Nicole: Yes, that's what he called it.

Callahan: Who else knew about the Bat Cave?

Nicole: Just his brother Brandon.

Callahan: Really? Do you know if he's been there before?

Nicole: Sure, he's been there a few times.

Callahan: Did Brandon have the code and key?

Nicole: I'm not sure about the code but Nicholas didn't want anyone to have a key.

Callahan: Thanks Nicole. Last question; where were you on the night of the murder.

Nicole: I was at home sleep...by myself.

Callahan walked Nicole out and returned to the Detective's office where the Lieutenant, Marcus and Logan were. Logan shook his head "that bitch is crazy. She actually thought that he loved her." "The question is, was she his protector or his killer" commented Marcus. Good job Callahan."

A.D. White

Chapter Eighteen
Day Of Reckoning

A few days later, Marcus had the driver Stephan Richardson brought to the Homicide office for an interview and also arranged for the receptionist Ashley Lake to come into the police station at the same time. Both arrived within a few minutes of each other and Ashley gave Stephan an evil glare. An officer showed them to the Detective's office on the second floor where Marcus and Logan awaited to interview Stephan. The lieutenant was in the observation deck. Detectives Callahan and Alverez were there to interview Ashley and Sergeant U was in that observation deck. The interviews or should I say interrogations began simultaneously.

Detective Alverez began Ashley's interview by advising her that the process was being videotaped, introducing herself and Detective Callahan.

Detective Alverez: Ashley, I have to advise you of your right to have an attorney during this interview and also your right to remain silent.

Ashley: Am I a suspect and do I need a lawyer?

Detective Callahan: At this point ma'am, everyone is a suspect and we're conducting this interview so that we can glean information to eliminate you as a suspect. It's your choice to seek legal counsel, but that would only delay the process at this point.

Ashley: (looked irritated) I'll waive my rights at this time. Let's just get this over with!

Detective Alverez: I'm sorry to be blunt but I have to ask this next question to everyone. Did you have anything to do with Mr. Lockett's murder?

Ashley: No, of course not.

Detective Alverez: Where were you on the night that he was murdered?

Ashley: I was at home asleep...by myself.

Detective Alverez: Can anyone verify that ma'am?

Ashley: How can anyone verify it if I said I was by myself Detective? (as she displayed her agitation)

Detective Alverez: So are you saying that you didn't leave your house at all that night?

Ashley: That's exactly what I'm saying.

Detective Callahan: Did you make any phone calls from your residence that night? That would tend to indicate your presence at home.

Ashley: No! (As she folded her arms)

Detective Alverez: Well Ashley, (as she opened the folder lying on the table) I have a copy of your phone log and it shows that you made a call at 1:20 am.

Ashley: Okay, I must have forgotten about that. What about it?

Detective Alverez: Did I mention that it was your cell phone, not your house phone? (As she folded her arms)

Ashley: (said nothing but had that "Oh Shit" look on her face)

Detective Callahan: What's significant about your cell phone is that not only do we know who you called but we also are aware of your location when the call was made.

Detective Alverez: You said that you were home alone, but this call was made two blocks away from Mr. Lockett's penthouse, shortly after he was murdered. Can you explain that?

Ashley: I'd like a lawyer at this time (as she looked down).

Meanwhile Marcus and Logan were interviewing Stephan Richardson.

Marcus: Stephan, did you have anything to do with Nicholas Lockett's murder?

Stephan: No!

Marcus: What is it exactly that you did for Nicholas Lockett?

Stephan: I was his driver.

Marcus: Were you his only driver or did he have two.

Stephan: No, I was the only one.

Marcus: When you finished driving Mr. Lockett for the day, what did you do with the Escalade.

Stephan: The car stayed with me at all times in case he called for me to pick him up or take him somewhere else.

Marcus: So basically, the vehicle was always in your possession?

Stephan: Yes.
Marcus: Where were you at 1:20 am on the night of the murder.

Stephan: I was at home, by myself.

Marcus: That's strange. Here in D.C. we have what we call the Automated Traffic Enforcement. Which means cameras that enforce red light violations and speeding.

Stephan: (had a confused look on his face)

Marcus: One of the things that I like to do on homicide cases is to check the traffic cameras in the area of the crime. You never know what you might see. Sometimes you can even develop witnesses. In this case, it appears that the Escalade that you say is always in your possession ran a red light four blocks from the scene and right after the murder occurred.

Marcus placed the picture of the Escalade running the red light on the table in front of Stephan

Logan: So can you see our dilemma now? If the vehicle is always in your possession, that means that there is a discrepancy with your story. You couldn't have been home at the time or the murder. It appears that you've been caught in a lie and if you lied about that, what else have you lied about?

Stephan: (Stephan started to answer but was interrupted by Logan).

Logan: You don't have to answer that. I asked that question for my amusement only. What you also lied about was being involved in this murder.

Stephan: Call me a lawyer.

Marcus/Logan: (Looked at each other and then responded) Okay...you're a lawyer.

Marcus: Good, because we don't need you to say anything else. We're going to do all the talking now and all I need you to do is listen.

There was a knock on the interview room door. Detective Callahan stuck his head in "Are you ready for her now?" Marcus motioned yes. Alverez and Callahan brought Ashley into the room and sat her beside Stephan Richardson. Marcus began "as I was just explaining to Stephan, you both have requested lawyers, therefore by law we cannot ask you anymore questions without your lawyer present. So I don't want you to say a word. All you need you to do is listen. I'm going to tell you what we know to be truth.

Marcus continued "On the night of Nicholas Lockett's murder, you Ashley said that you were home alone. But that wasn't true. You put on that flimsy disguise, entered the building and went to the penthouse that you said you had never been to. We know that was a lie because shortly after you murdered him, you left the building, walked two blocks away and called Stephan to pick you up. He was a few blocks away and in his haste, ran a red light." Marcus pointed to the picture that was already on the table. "This makes Stephan an accomplice to your crime.

Callahan began "on the night of this heinous and repugnant crime, we have a picture of what we believe to be the murderer disguised with a big coat and hat walk past the concierge's desk and onto the elevator." Callahan removed the picture from the folder and placed it on the table in front of Ashley "even though the picture is not definitive, we know that it's you. The killer inadvertently stepped into some of the blood on the floor and left a partial foot print. There was enough of the foot print to determine that it belonged to a woman's size nine shoe and I've been told that you in fact wear a size nine.

"This is crazy" blurted Ashley in disgust. "What reason would I have to kill Nicholas Lockett?" "I'm glad you asked" replied Marcus. "We wondered about that ourselves. What in the world could Nicholas Lockett have done to you for you to murder him in such a violently passionate way? When Detective Steele interviewed you, you claimed that Nicholas Lockett tried to rape you. In fact, I believe that he didn't attempt to rape, he actually did rape you. And you Stephan felt guilty or Ashley blackmailed you because you stood by and let it happen. Shortly after that, the plan was concocted to kill Nicholas Lockett. You had one major obstacle; how to get into the penthouse that needed a key and code and without the concierge seeing you. That's where Stanley the concierge comes into play. It didn't go unnoticed that both Stanley's and Stephan's last names are Richardson. It was easy to verify that you're brothers. Stanley listed Stephan as his brother on his employment paper work when he was hired as the concierge. He provided you with the key and code and was suspiciously absent from his desk when Ashley entered and exited the building.

There was a ten thousand dollar deposit into Stanley's bank account a week before the murder. He was obviously paid for his participation.

Last but not least, during the interview with Detective Steele, Ashley stated that she knew sooner or later that someone would slash Nicholas Lockett's throat. We never released the fact that his throat was slashed. Only that the manner of death was by a stabbing. The family didn't even have that information. The only person that could have known that was the killer. Marcus then picked up a pen from the interview table and tossed it to Ashley. It was no surprise to Marcus that she caught it with her left hand. Marcus then said "oh, and the killer was left handed."

This was a premeditated murder and both of you are under arrest. Presently, both of your houses are being searched for evidence. He looked at Ashley "I'm not sure if you were dumb enough to keep the clothes that you wore or the murder weapon, but if you did, we'll find it." Marcus removed his trusty hand sanitizer from his jacket pocket and squirted some on his hands, rubbing them together.

"Fuck this" said Stephan. "This was her idea, not mine. She made me do it." Ashley looked at Stephan with amazement and disgust "shut the hell up, all they have is a theory." She threw her hands up in the air "you can't be this fucking dumb. PLEASE STOP TALKING." "I'm not going to jail for you" Stephan shouted. "Too late for that now" Marcus mumbled.

"Both of you stand up. You're under arrest" said Marcus. Logan placed the handcuffs on Stephan and Alverez placed the handcuffs on Ashley. "I can't believe you" said Ashley as she looked at Stephan. Then she tried to kick him as Detective Alverez pulled her away. Ashley lost her composure "Fuck all of you." "Wow" said Logan. "Do you kiss yo mama with that mouth" he jokingly asked. "I'm sure she uses it for more than that" mumbled Alverez.

As Alverez and Logan walked them to the cell block area to be processed, Stanley the concierge was coming through the door. His eyes lit up as he saw them in handcuffs. Logan smiled and asked him "remember what I said about going to the pokey?" Stanley sighed heavily and said "I didn't know they were going to kill him. I was paid for the key and code and to leave my desk and look the other way, but I had no idea that she was going to kill him. She was supposed to show up at the door and black mail him. I didn't sign up for no murder. Stanley just shook his head in disgust as he realized that his whole life had just fell apart.

Marcus said to Stanley "come here and put your hands behind your back. You're under arrest for conspiracy to commit murder. "All of you are going to jail for a long time because of your greed. Ashley looked up "I've got news for you Detective. Greed rules the world." Marcus replied "When greed rules the world, no one profits."

Chapter Nineteen
Cleanliness Is Next To Godliness

After they finished processing the arrests, the entire squad met back in their office. They sat and reflected on the case. "Good work people, this was truly a team effort" said the lieutenant. "I echo the lieutenant's sentiment. As usual, great job" said Sergeant U. Logan leaned back in his chair "yeah, I couldn't have done this without the rest of you" he joked. "I'm glad that we could assist you" sarcastically remarked Detective Callahan. "I guess it's not just money that's the root of all evil. We can add revenge to that list also" said Marcus. "It's amazing what people try to get away with" said Logan. "My grandmother used to say that every closed eye ain't sleep and every goodbye ain't gone (Marcus seemed to be reminiscing).

The custodian that cleans the building was named Joe Braxton. He was an older black man with balding hair. Dressed in brown slacks with a white button up shirt. Brown shoes that were scuffed and looked as if they had seen better days. He had been working there for years and all the detectives loved to talk to him because he had a way with words. Mr. Braxton happened to be cleaning the Detective's office at this time and couldn't help but hear their conversation.

"My mother used to say the same thing" he told Marcus. "You know that the stripture says that everything that we do in the dark will come out in the light." Detective Callahan asks inquisitively "stripture?" Mr. Braxton replies "yeah, you know the good book." Callahan smiled "oh you mean scripture." "That's what I said, stripture" responded Joe. This amused everyone in the squad. Logan interjected "you know Callahan; you're not the only person here that speaks proper English." Callahan replied "really Logan? You're an enigma." Mr. Braxton stopped dead in his tracks "whoa Detective Steele, you gonna let that white man call you that?" Logan laughed "I'm gonna let him get away with it this time. He's saying that I'm difficult to understand." "Whoo, okay, cause I thought he was calling you something else." The entire squad broke out in laughter.

"There's one thing that I don't understand" Logan said to Marcus. "What's that" he replied. "Brandon Lockett lied about not knowing that his brother had the Penthouse. Why?" "Because he's a compulsive liar and that's his nature" responded Marcus. Logan shook his head "that makes no sense to me. Why lie when you have nothing to hide?" Marcus thought for a few seconds and asked "have you ever heard of the Scorpion and the Frog?" "No, enlighten me" responded Logan.

"A scorpion and a frog meet on the bank of a stream and the scorpion asks the frog to carry him across on its back. The frog asks, "How do I know you won't sting me?" The scorpion says, "Because if I do, I will die too." The frog is satisfied, and they set out, but in midstream, the scorpion stings the frog. The frog feels the onset of paralysis and starts to sink, knowing they both will drown, but has just enough time to gasp "Why?" The scorpion replies "It's my nature."

Marcus stood up "well, I'm going to call it a night." Sergeant U stood up and said "let's all celebrate our win down at the Drunken Skunk (the local bar that many cops frequented). I'm buying." "I'm in" said the lieutenant. "Me too" replied Callahan. "If you buying, I'm drinking" said Logan as he looked at Alverez. "What about you. You joining us" he asked. She looked into his eyes, contemplating the answer, then shook her head no "not tonight, I'm a little tired."

Everyone looked at Marcus "nah, not tonight. I've got somewhere I've got to be. I'll take a rain check though." The lieutenant, the sergeant and Callahan walked out. As Alverez was walking out, Logan looked at her and said "hey, you got a minute? Wanna talk to you about something." "I got a minute" she replied. "Good night" said Marcus as he was walking out.

Now that they were alone, Logan looked at Alverez and said "I've been doing some thinking." "Yeah, about what, dare I ask" replied Alverez. "About us" he replied. Alverez sighed "look Logan, I like you. I really do. You're a smart guy, tall dark and handsome but we both know that you have never learned to be true to one woman." "'That may be true up to now" replied Logan, "but I can change for the right person." "And you think that I'm the right person" she replied? "I do Al. All I need is the chance to prove it to you" as he reached over and placed his hand over hers.

Alverez took a minute to respond "we gotta start off with small steps Logan, very small steps." "I can do that" he replied. Logan continued "let me take you out to dinner tomorrow. A good meal and sparkling conversation." "Sounds good" she replied as they both got up and started walking out. "Wear that black nightie that I know you've got," Logan said jokingly. Alverez laughed "see Logan, that's what I'm talking about, you play too much man!" "Just a little joke. You look good in anything that you wear" said Logan. You could hear Alverez saying "what am I getting myself into" as they left the building.

Marcus pulled up to the hospice and parked his vehicle. He slowly entered the building and took the stairs up to the second floor. As he entered the ward, he stopped at the nurse's station. "Hi Marcus" said the nurse. She's in and out today. She'll be glad to see you though." Marcus smiled and continued to room 2048. He stopped at the door and saw her resting peacefully. He wondered if he should go in and wake her or let her sleep.

Just then her eyes opened. Marcus walked over to the bed. "Is that you Marcus" she asked. "Yeah Ma, It's me." "You look just like your daddy, God rest his soul." Marcus smiled "I've been told that before. He must have been a handsome man" he joked as he held her hand.

"I'm a little thirsty. Would you mind getting me some water? "I don't mind" Marcus replied as he left the room to get it. He returned with the water and straw and walked back to her bedside. "Is that you Marcus" his mother asked again? "Yeah Ma, it's me. How you doing today" he asked? "Much better now that my baby boy is here to see me." Marcus smiled and kissed her on the forehead." "Did you wash your hands today" she asked. "Yes Mom, I did" as he smiled, "I never forget to do that. You always told me that cleanliness was next to Godliness." "I'm so proud of you Marcus." He smiled "I love you Mom."

A.D. White

www.adwhite.net

Also by A.D. White:

A Killing In D.C., The Chronicles Of Detective Marcus Rose (Volume One)

Your feedback is greatly appreciated. Please leave a comment at my website, www.adwhite.net

Editors:

Dolores W. Allen
Rosalind N. White

Cover Illustration by D.J. Jackson, HF Productions

Made in the USA
Middletown, DE
29 June 2021